Alexander Lookup

The Soldier of the People or the World's Deliverer

Alexander Lookup

The Soldier of the People or the World's Deliverer

ISBN/EAN: 9783337051761

Printed in Europe, USA, Canada, Australia, Japan

Cover: Foto ©Andreas Hilbeck / pixelio.de

More available books at **www.hansebooks.com**

THE

SOLDIER

OF

THE PEOPLE;

OR,

THE WORLD'S DELIVERER.

A ROMANCE

BY ALEXANDER LOOKUP,

Author of "Our Hero Abroad," "Adventures of an Interesting Young Man," &c.

NEW-YORK & LONDON:
KENNEDY, PUBLISHER, 483 BROADWAY.
1860.

THE

SOLDIER OF THE PEOPLE;

OR, THE

WORLD'S CAPTAIN.

BOOK I.

CHAPTER I.

Scene.—A park in the city of Washington, within view of the Capitol. Enter Ladies of the French, Austrian, Russian and other embassies at Washington. Lady Magog reading newspaper

Lady Magog. O the startling advertisement that is here !
Lady Gog. What ?
Lady Magog. (Reads.) 'On the 4th July, I, Hercules Power, will be in Washington, and from the Capitol steps will, at 12 o'clock, publish forth the everlasting, rational, natural, profitable law for the whole world, the Enlightened Law, the best law for all classes ; also will set forth a plan for an immediate Diamond United States of the Globe ; first of America and afterwards of all mankind ; also will explain

my intended expedition to Europe to liberate the enslaved People's from the power of the contemptuous political gamesters; also I shall introduce the Queen Justitia, Heaven's prosy, to the Sovereign Citizens, and more than forty Sovereign Queens, deputies of the Sovereign People of different States.'

Lady Gog. O dear, dear, what a perfect thunder clap of an advertisement.

Lady Magog. Don't let it confound you, ladies. We shall have capital use for all our ingenuity, I tell you, to meet and defeat the Goliath of Enlightened Law.

[Enter newsboys calling extra. Ladies buy paper and read.

' General Power left this morning for Washington to inaugurate the Diamond Republic.'

Lady Magog. Something immediate we must do !

Lady Gog. Truly, no hope for the powers of Europe, nor for any other power, if raptured General Power gets any headway in America, in inaugurating his Diamond Republic of Mankind as he denominates it.

[Enter Old Time, who, planting his hour glass on the ground, leans contemplatively on his scythe.

Old Time. (Speaks in soliloquy.) Lo, I'm the reaper
Of all the world heretofore, yet am I Old Time,
Good for innumerable years to come.

[The timorous women of fashion for the first time get a glimpse of Old Time.

Lady Magog. Look, a spectre !

[Ladies turn white—two of them faint in arms of servants.

Lady Gog. 'Tis Old Time himself, or some one who affects his disastrous semblance.

Lady Magog. No doubt a fellow sent by plaguy Power
To sadden us with presage of disaster,
And fill us up with stagnant weight of thought,
And melancholy that invites mishap.

Lady Gog. Beshrew him sinister as a raven.

Lady Magog. That hops foreboding thwart the traveler's path.

Lady Gog. Beshrew him ! a knave, I warrant him, and intending a threat in the attitude now assumed. Doubtless some nameless vagrant—come hither to aid Hercules Power's millennial inauguration.

Lady Magog. Get up immediate troupe of furies, and thereupon tear Hercules Power.

Lady Gog. O let us about it, for I have great fear of aspiring General Power getting a headway, which if he does, it is all over with particular great powers throughout the world.

Old Time. Very natural fear, considering you stand like thunder clouds toward the Sovereign Masses soon to be raptured to unity; soon to vote the right sort of law and government by universal plaudits to the heaven that clips mankind everlastingly around.

Lady Magog. So, in order to be prepared to meet and defeat upstart democratic Power, hire we several cankered old women, and open, by their means, a broadside of satire, ridiculing and nullifying his popular efforts.

Lady Gog. Good, get a troop of furies and lead them on to the attack of the democrat at the moment of his contemplated millennial inauguration.

> [Old Time never in all his irksome pilgrimage for a moment in the same position, appears to the timid ladies to make a threatening demonstration with his scythe.

Lady Gog. Ho, call my Lord Ambassador Gog !
[Exeunt Servants.

Lady Magog. Ho, summon my Lord Ambassdor Magog !
[Exeunt more Lackeys.

[Immediately rush upon the scene of action Lord
Gog and Lord Magog, severally armed with a club,
followed by Lackeys who surround Old Time and
menace him.

Lord Gog. What are you doing here, you vile old tallow-
face ?

Old Time. I am thinking of God's patience.

Lord Gog. How, ye rascal ?   His patience about what ?

Old Time. Waiting the matter of six thousand years to
see this world, plagued with Tyrants and their inventions,
put right and straight; giving capital opportunity to innumerable statesmen, and at the end having to interfere
Himself in the all important matter of social rectification.

Lord Gog. Interfere, you scoundrel ! what d'ye mean by
that ?

Old Time. Commander General Power, Enlightenment's
chief apostle, as I understand, is arrived !

Lord Magog. Villain, are ye come hither to play the evil
prophet, and hang like an ominous comet in unclouded sky,
to craftily conjure up a popular commotion.   Who sent ye
hither, ye knave ?

Old Time. No one !

Magog. Ye lie, fellow !

Lord Gog. Ye're confederate with Power.

Magog. Allied to notorious republican upstart,
Power, so popular now with the people.

Old Time. No, I am Power's herald and forerunner,

Magog. Enlightenment's self-boasted apostle, whom tho
people dub their champion ?

Old Time. Praised be God ! The people at length united on enlightened champion ? Praised be God ! Then the millennium's nigh ! O praised be God !

Magog. There, take that, ye old caitiff !

[Hits him with club.

Gog. Take that for more improvement of your manners.

[Hits him, too, with club.

Old. Time. Help an old man ! Help, some one in mercy, help !

Enter Donald.

Donald. Drop your coward work; I say, drop your coward work ! What are ye about ? Drop belaboring an old man, ye unnatural brutes !

[Donald hits the Ambassadors on the back. They turn on Donald, while the Lackeys pummel the old man.

Old Time. Help ! help ! help !

Donald. Ay, in a jiffy !

[Blows a whistle. Thereupon enter young men of the Army of the Sun.

Magog. Who are ye, so saucy ?

1st Young Man. We serve rapturous master.

2d Young Man. Commander General Power.

Magog. More of the notorious democratic upstart's hirelings, eh ? begone ! caitiffs, begone !

1st Young Man. Not without more physical reason !

[Upon that, the young men, severally donning a helmet and plume of gold, which adds considerably to their stature, Gog and Magog and the Lackeys take precipitately to their heels, followed by the Ladies of the Embassies, screaming and shrieking in affected fear for their lives.

Donald. Come on !

1st *Young Man.* We'll fight you individually any way you choose it.   [Exeunt.

CHAPTER II.

Scene.—A street in Washington city.

Enter Magnus Sham and company, political chessmen and their numerous friends, some habited as drovers with great top coats and devilish snaky whips; others as butchers, with blue gowns and white aprons spotted over with blood; all large burly men, Magnus himself presenting the respectable proportion of a sugar hogshead.

Magnus Sham. How to stop mighty General Power is the urgent question.

Sham. Why, if he is as they give out, all powerful, impossible to stop him.

Magnus Sham. Ah, Enlightenment, that's the savior of the people, will be our death stroke.

Sham. The sovereigns raptured up to diamond unity, farewell we political speculators; farewell coercive drovers and butchers of the State.

    [Enter Drovers cracking whips and driving a weary drooping herd of poor creatures, clad in sheep skins.,

Magnus Sham. Drive them in the shambles, here !

    [Magnus points out the place of sacrifice to the political and other victims. Immediately all the herd make a great outcry.

Herd. Magnus, Magnus, we voted for you, but vote for you no more if you forsake us in now urgent strait.

[Great outcry of the Herd continued.

Magnus Sham. O my friends, there's my hand! To help you out of difficulty I'm never slow.

Drovers. Fy, Magnus, to give so many free passes out of their trouble to our legitimate cattle. Fy, Magnus!

Magnus Sham. The rest I don't know; drive them in and butcher them without pity.

[Drovers drive the rest into the political shambles. Butchers whetting their knives, follow the drovers inside. Anon, runs forth Poor Bankrupt very much frightened.

Poor Bankrupt. It's real butchering they're after.

Magnus Sham. What, bold knave, broken away from the ring bolt?

Poor Bankrupt. I see no reason in having my throat cut.

Magnus Sham. Rebel! traitor! mutineer! lawless villain!

Poor Bankrupt. Rebel! traitor! lawless villain! for objecting to having my throat cut, or the same thing, natural hereditary sovereign rights trampled by Sham and Company. Truly, you're a reasonable man!

Magnus Sham. Thou art my prisoner!

Poor Bankrupt. When you catch me.

[Exit Bankrupt, running.

Magnus Sham. Pursue! pursue!
O'ertake and bring him back and slaughter him.

[Exeunt Drovers and Butchers in determined hurry followed by Magnus Sham and Company, in a **fuming excitement.**

BOOK II.

CHAPTER I.

Scene.—The steps of the capitol at Washington.

Enter Lords Gog and Magog, and Ladies Gog and Magog and other ladies, evidently excited and worried, followed by Lackeys and others.

Lord Magog. There's money! Go, and with liberal gratuities bring shoulder-hitters and rowdies to assemble at the proper moment, and spoil democratic upstart Power's contemplated millennial inauguration.

Lackeys. Ay, my lord.   [Exeunt Lackeys.

Lady Magog. Those who came to the assistance of the old villain assailing us in the park, were hirelings of the popular upstart Power, part of his rapturous voluntary force, as he calls them, now arrived to participate in the millennial celebration.

Lady Gog. Thank heaven, or otherwise the consequences were direful, they're no more than a force of sanguine asses, raptured blockheads, kicking up heels for their own especial, silly amusement; nobody else.

Lady Magog. Come away and get haggard creatures to open battery of venomed darts on democratic upstart Power.

Lord Magog. Come, Lord Gog, let us disguise and put ourselves at the head of the shoulder-hitters.

[Exeunt Lords and Ladies.
Enter Citizens.

1st Cit. O the amazing news!

2d Cit. What, sir? what?

1st Cit. General Power has announced in the newspapers the forthcoming inauguration of Enlightened Diamond Republic.

3d Cit. And what is more wonder—

1st Cit. The appearance of Justitia, the Queen of Heaven's Proxy, Celestial Justice herself, to publish from the capitol steps her message to the united Sovereign Citizens.

3d Cit. How now, General Power and his staff !

> [Enter General Power and his staff, namely General Eagle, General Trump, and other officers in full uniform, greeting Honorable Senators and Representatives, entering from the other side. Citizens gather round and attentively listen.

Gen. P. Honorable representatives of congress, as do all legislators, you exist in consequence of weakness and distraction of the sovereign people. No other reason.

1st Senator. No doubt, Mr. Power! no doubt !

Gen. P. It is my rapturous part, as the advocate of Enlightenment and Enlightened law, to show how to perfectly unite the Sovereign People, not of our unrivalled country only, but of all the haggard world beyond.

1st Senator. Ha! ha! ha ! you're an extraordinary man.

2d Senator. Anxious of being esteemed a span exceeding Hercules ! Ha ! ha ! ha !

Gen. P. Who are the authors of the sovereign citizens' weakness and distraction? Perhaps you do not know it, gentlemen. It behooves then I do enlighten you at once.

Senators. O ho ! ho ! ho !

Gen. P. First the crafty, hypocritical getters up of the superstition of the cross, which is the religion of Jesus' crucifiers, the Pharisees, never Jesus' own, who correctly promulgated love and light, as they are in God for the means of salvation, that by its reptile discrepancies, and by its creed of tyrannous bigotry, weakens and distracts, so proving itself incapable to fulfill the demands of enlightened future.

1st Senator. Indeed! Ha! ha! ha! ha! That's new!

Gen. P. I announce Enlightenment according to heaven, God's surrounding standard, to be the true son of God, the perfect, rapturous Redeemer, designed by the Almighty Father, to magnetically elevate, rapture and unite the Sovereign People, like sunshine everlasting, and, in doing so, I blast the unworthy serpent of superstition, splitting the citizens into distracted sects and parties, giving them up a prey to every cajoling tyrant, from Emperor down to pot-house politician.

1st Senator. Why, you don't mean to reflect on us, do you?

Gen. P. O, by no means, gentlemen, only on the superstition, giving the people to worship bigotry and misery in lieu of Enlightenment, of all the popular mind, by every rational means, from earliest years in Rational Universities, otherwise God of Nature's universal Catholic churches, schools and colleges combined of the whole people. Enlightenment, imbuing all like ineffable God, soon changes the world into one harmonious, rapturous, brotherly unit like the glorious onward and omnipotent planet itself.

1st Senator. But, how, if your Enlightenment modify, or upset the present political state?

Gen. Power. State! none in the world, but God and the universal, enlightened, united sovereign citizens. State! Where is state of any legitimacy but that which inaugurates Heaven's kingdom, which every one has been praying for since he was a child? State! The Sovereign People, made one by Enlightenment, realize the greatest state imaginable, resplendent heaven for all the enlightened future of the

planet; happiness, opulence, and unity for all the magnetically united millions of sovereign citizens who tread the raptured ship, whereof God Omnipotent is Captain.

1st Senator. Sir, you speak with a thundering deal of
command.

Gen. Power. Enlightenment commands. Nothing save
enlightenment has legitimate right to command in the world,
which owes itself to God wholly enlightened. Enlightenment is God's redeemer for all mankind. Enlightenment,
or imbuing with God's mind and principles according to His
surrounding standard of Heaven, is the new Messiah, to re-
claim by Enlightened Law and Government, the sovereign
people out of Egypt, and out of the withering power of
deadly bigots and despots. No more meteor like Napoleons,
lurid fire-balls, betraying a generation to its ruin; but rapturous Herculeses of perfection achieved through light alone,
developing in heavenly shape, beauty, truth and grace. To
all the self-interested and nefarious teachers of superstition,
the seconds of tyrants, who have sold the world to its masters, I say, I am armed with God's perfect weapon of light,
to frighten the souls of the enemies of mankind; to discover
all hypocrites and pretenders to government; to elevate the
world and complete it through enlightenment, according to
God's open Scriptures and rapturous surrounding standard of
heaven.

1st Senator. Why, now, sir, what has started you like a
meteor upon so extraordinary erratic mission?

Gen. Power. It is tyrannous oppression that hath made
me so enlightened warlike. Oppression from the government's agents; oppression from your exorbitant courts, and
their mercenary officers. I am become the archangel,
scourge of dragon governments, the resplendent terror of all
the icy powers, to moderate them down, and to change hag-

gard humanity, like light upon the darkened waters, into the serene mirror of heaven itself.

3d Senator. What is your name?

Gen. Power. Hercules Power!

3d Senator. Indeed, sir! Sometimes we hear of you as General Power, though you are not on our army list.

Hercules Power. Nevertheless, I am about to take command of a mighty army; a voluntary army of the all-powerful, Enlightened, United People, that will briefly estop endless rent and taxation; dry up exorbitant government whether federal or municipal; and re-model the country rapturous and natural, right and straight; putting the ship round for the New Universal Supernal California at every sovereign man's door, immediately ravished by Enlightened Law.

1st Senator. Ha, we have read accounts something like this in the newspapers.

Hercules Power. Behold the future capitol of the world!

1st Congressman. Where?

Hercules Power. There, gentlemen! (pointing to the sky,) The everlasting heaven!

1st Congressman. Ha!

Hercules Power. Ay, gentlemen, a capitol not to oppress the earth, but perpetually rapture it.

1st Congressman. Ha, indeed!

Hercules Power. Ay, gentlemen, and there reigns eternally at that capitol a queen who is about to translate herself hither, yea, take up her residence upon every foot of the habitable globe.

2d Congressman. Indeed, sir! her name?

Hercules Power. Justice, handmaid of God!

2d Congressman. Ha, ha, ha!

Hercules Power. Ay, 'tis true.

1st Congressman. O, sir, that is quite supererogatory labor ! we have already established Justice sufficiently in the courts.

Hercules Power. But she is gratuitous and universal Justice without courts, save one Enlightened self-supporting Court of the county, otherwise God's court for social perfection, for rapturous and satisfactory Justice at the enlightened start. She is Justice without horrid and exorbitant tax grinding courts ; oppressive creatures borrowed of Europe's tyrants. She is Justice in accordance with Nature. She is Justice as ordained by Supreme God Almighty

1st Congressman. We'll not have her !

2d Congressman. We don't want to see her !

Hercules Power. But the enlightened People may, gentlemen.

1st Senator. We shall not admit her to the Senate.

1st Congressman. Nor to the house of Representatives.

Hercules Power. Yet she fills heaven, Justice doth ; and I doubt not, will be welcomed on earth, and especially in free enlightened America.

1st Congressman. We'll not have her, as we've said already.

Hercules Power. That, gentlemen, is for the Enlightened Sovereign Citizens to say, not for you, nor for I. At all events, it can do nobody any harm to look on diamond perfection in Justitia, representing the Queen of Heaven, and therefore I shall prepare to present her to you at the earliest opportunity.

[Exeunt Senators and Representatives.

[Enter a deputation of Mechanics, introduced by Hercules Power's friend, General Diamond.

Gen. Power. Welcome, gentlemen !

1st Mechanic. We must needs be by Enlightenment's Apostle.

2d Mechanic. Yet, O, Commander Power, we fear to meddle with what we don't understand

Gen. Power. Seek Enlightenment, that will give you understanding enough.

Gen. Diamond.   With Enlightenment,
The world becomes an immediate heavenly unit;
Splendid, harmonious like an entire diamond,
And raptured onward as the omnipotent planet.

Gen. Power. You must know that a great part of the machinery of government, the world over, is a counterfeit heaven, elevated by bigots and despots over the Sovereign People to eclipse the perfect, true, superlative Heaven on Earth of the ineffable, universal God, the Author of our being.

1st Mechanic. Read us a few paragraphs from the Enlightened Bible, that Light and Rapture your pupils are writing for the People's grand magnetic union.

     [General Power withdraws a book from his pocket, and reads.

Gen. Power. The soil is God's property, a part of the rapturous heavens. It cannot be taxed. How it came to be taxed at first was all by Cæsars and Saints in collusion.

Mechanics. Hurrah, Light! Hurrah, Rapture! Hurrah Enlightenment! Hurrah, General Power, or enlightened popular strength and freedom, the capital result of Enlightenment!

Gen. Power. Ay, gentlemen, Enlightenment were no better than the old superstition, except for the many diamond gifts it brings.

1st Mechanic. What, O, General Power?

2d Mechanic.   Altho' we can't imagine,
Yet thy exceeding rapturous eye and mien,
Like open sky, leads us to hope fair day.

Gen. Power. No better than the haggard, ragged, worn out superstition, if it did not bring——

1st Mechanic. What?

Gen. Power.　　　　Everything;
Unity, happiness, opulence, content,
Prosperity to everybody without end;
Enlightened royalty to all mankind,
A diamond world accomplished by enlightenment.

1st Mechanic. No doubt, O, General Power! Enlightenment is the modern, rational, true and perfect Re-
　　deemer!

2d Mechanic. The immeasurable mountain prospect opened Doth buoy us up with rapture off our feet—
Proceed, O, General Power!

[Enter a poor Bankrupt.]

Bankrupt. I am unfortunate, but, I suppose, I must bear my cross like other unlucky speculators.

Com. Power. How did this cross happen to you?

Bankrupt. By too great confidence in paper.

Com. Power. O, you leant on a paper redeemer?

Bankrupt. Ay, sir!

Com. Power. Paper redeemer! Pretty thing to keep a man in hope. Pretty faith is paper redeemer to offer en-lightened public!

Bankrupt. I'm in a heap of trouble. O God, deliver me!
[Runs and returns.

Com. Power. God would, sir, but cannot, because, being out of your paper redeemer, you have accepted to bear a cross, in lieu of an enlightened heart.

Bankrupt. Sir, O you do startle me by your original in-dependent manner of thinking.

Com. Power. Attend to me! I am Hercules Power, who

hath undertook an enlightened war upon all crosses. See God's standard, Enlightenment, that put's all the world right and straight at the start, in natural, and rapturous mode. Will you join it?

Bankrupt. Ay, aught that will put me up again in hope.

Com. Power. Enlightenment will do it! Your cross and all crosses, however they are got, are quite needless, and by enlightenment can be prevented. Come with me!

> [Enter Magnus Sham and Company, and Drovers and Butchers, the former flourishing whips, the latter brandishing knives. They all rush on Poor Bankrupt.

Magnus Sham. Seize him! Traitor! rebel! mutineer

Donald. Off notorious tyrants and cutthroat encumbrances!

> [Donald shakes them off Poor Bankrupt.

Gen. Power. Unhand him! Every man Sovereign by Enlightenment!

> [General Power draws his sword; young soldiers of the Army of the Sun rush between with drawn swords. Magnus' friends drop their weapons in despair.

SONG.

Bravo, General Power!
Rapturing us by Enlightenment
To heaven full of splendor,
And diamond unity and content.
Bravo, General Power!

Magnus Sham. O!

> [Magnus succumbs back in the arms of his friends.

Drover. What's the matter with Mr. Magnus?

Magnus Sham.   Friends,

I'm suddenly indisposed, so carry me
Home to my possible death-bed.

[Exeunt Magnus, &c

[Enter quietly and unobserved, Old Time with scythe
and hour-glass. He seats himself down on the
steps of the Capitol, within the august shadow of
the grand Corinthian columns. The same moment
all eyes are riveted upon the extraordinary old hero.

1st Mechanic. Who's that?
2d Mechanic. I think Old Time,
Or individual of his wizard semblance.

Old Time. (Soliloquizing.) He comes of a capital stock,
does Hercules Power, the rational friend of the people, among
whom rank as pre-eminent, Paine and Franklin, who, persecu-
ted and despairing for existence under despots, migrated to
America.   He has in this enlightened age of progress, under
favor of Enlightened Public Opinion, lately gained such
addition, that they begin to entitle him, Commander General
Power.

Hercules Power. To every one of you, gentlemen, Enlightenment brings royal portion ; all privileges that hedge a king
against contiguity of vulgar misfortune ; every one endowed
with a part of the raptured ship ; and no more heartless
sheriff to sacrifice you ; one of the universal, all-powerful,
sovereign brotherhood, who laugh to scorn the now ghostly
Cæsars waning like moon before the morn's resplendent
dawn.

Gen. Diamond. O. universal Enlightened Sovereign
People, as oft as any needless trouble happens to you, think
on Commander General Power ; but, above all, think on one
another, and bear a hand to powerfully enforce one another
in your enlightened war upon crosses and on all withering

superstition, and on all bigots and despots, whether they defy you as in Europe, or cajole you as in the United States.

Mechanics. Long live General Diamond! - Bravo, Enlightened Law and Government, akin to that of Nature's Author! Bravo, the complete Diamond Republic! Long live General Power!

> [No sooner Old Time hears vociferated the name of General Power by the raptured citizens, than leaping to his feet, and throwing away his scythe, and knocking over his hour-glass, he rushes up to the General, and looking him a moment in the face, then clasps him passionately.

Old Time. I have found him, I have found him, heaven be thanked! found him, for whom I've pined an exceeding time. [Embraces him.

Gen. Power. How now, my old chap? Found whom?

Old Time. The diamond Hero of Enlightenment!

Mechanics. Who?

Old Time. A soldier, General Power, Before all hitherto; the people's brother! No proud upstart oppressor!

Mechanics. Bravo, General Power! Bravo, Old Time, enlightened Power's sire!

> [Old Time again embraces the General.

Old Time. I have found him! I have found him! Heaven be thanked! Found him more opulent than mines of Golconda, Enlightenment's apostle who'll change the world like one resplendent diamond.

Mechanics. Bravo, Old Time!

Old Time. Old? Gentlemen, I'm young Time now. I take a new start from this rapturous epoch.

SONG.

By the Rapturous Mechanics, and young men of the Army
of the Sun.

Bravo, old chap!
No more ahead of the world,
Content to play the child;
And dally, laugh, and chat;
Laugh and chat.
And dally, laugh, and chat,
Like a good old chap;
Like a good, good, good
Old chap.

[They slap the ancient gentleman on the back, and
surround and otherwise caress him. He seems
very much pleased with their attentions.

Old Time. Hurrah, Rapturous General Power is the
enlightened soldier the world needs.

Gen. Power. Truce to your flattery, Father Time!

1st Mechanic. Time's flattery's always merited, General.

Old Time. Faith, thou'rt my hearty. To embrace thee
something involuntarily draws me,
) thou magnet, General Power!

[Old Time again clasps the General.

Gen. Power. Much obliged to you for this affectionate
hug, old Mr. Time. If you bear light, there's no other can
plant a wrinkle.

Mechanics. Bravo, Old Time!
Bravo, young giant Power, Old Time's recruit!

[Young men of the army of the Sun, pick up Old
Time's scythe, and offer to fix it again upon his
shoulder.

Mechanics. Old Time, here is your scythe, you had forgot.

Old Time. I'll have none of it, I'm young Time. Now, bring me blossoms! bring me wine! bring me genial woman-kind! I'll straight marry; settle me down, and rear an all-powerful family of children.

> [General Power takes Old Time's arm to escort him. Young men of the army of the Sun, and the Rapturous Mechanics follow suit.

Gen. Power.   Come, Father Time!
Choose you my poor house for your residence.

Old Time. But I have a large family, soon forthcoming, General!

Gen. Power. I have thought of that, Father Time. Hard by, is a Rapturous University where all the neighborhood's taught in the capital creed of Nature's God, Author of the universal heavens.

Young Men. What shall we do with your scythe, then, Mr. Time?

Old Time. Hang it! I'll none of it.

Gen. Power.   Hang up Time's scythe
With venerable memorials on the wall
For marvel of the future generations.

Old Time. Ay, hang it up! anything, so you put it out of sight! Don't any more speak of scythe in the enlight-ened rapturous time, the forthcoming millennium.

> [Young men play and sport with Time's scythe.

Old Time. Guide me to rapturous University. I'm im-patient to see what provision is made for education of the future, forthcoming innumerable family. Guide me to Rap-turous University, General.

1st Young Man. Come, Father Time!

Join arm in arm young men of the Army of the Sun
and rapturous Mechanics singing.

SONG.

By young men of the Army of the Sun and Raptured
Mechanics.

Come away and joyfully take life,
Hitherto haggard Time has dropt his scythe;
Join our raptured army of Enlightened youth,
Come away and let us joyfully livé;
Let us joyful, joyful live.

[Excunt young men and raptured mechanics singing.

Enter Citizens.

1st Citizen. What's the news? why are you all on high
waves of excitation?

2d Citizen. O, you must know old Time is come amongst
us!

1st Citizen. What, Old Time?

2d Citizen. Ay!

1st Citizen. No thanks to him, a lukewarm customer whom
we can neither call enemy nor friend.

2d Citizen. But he hath put away his scythe, Old Time
hath. O, he hath grown to be a youth, Old Time hath,
since the haggard laws are to be got rid of.

1st Citizen. Old Time has veritably come amongst us
then?

2d Citizen. Rather, to drop figures; humanity has now
fallen upon its millennium, a long summer, ripening into a
mellow autumn.   [Exeunt.

CHAPTER II.

A public park and promenade. General Hercules Power with his friends descending the front steps of his house. Enter Lady Gog and Lady Magog, and other ladies of the embassies.

Lady Magog. There is General Power and his staff. At him !

Lady Gog. Disgrace him before his officers, call him infamous names.

1st Hag. Ay, we'll call names, and make him blush up to his eyes.

Lady Magog. At him ! Take him systematically to pieces like an anatomical subject. Disgrace him before his officers. Don't leave him a stitch of character wherewith to aspire to any respectability again.

    [The Hags severally stick out their fingers at General
      Power.

All the Hags. O ho, ho, ho, ho, ho, ho !

1st Hag. See at the gnat straining to be an elephant !

2d Hag. See at the would-be lion !

All the Hags. O ho, ho, ho, ho, ho, ho !

Gen. Eagle. See, Scandal with her caustic tongue,
And finger of disdain.

Gen. Power. Ho, Donald !

            Enter Donald.

Donald. Ay, sir, here !

Gen. Power. If you know any likely young men for Hymen's capital knot, bring them hither right away, Donald.

Donald. Ay, ay, General.   [Exit Donald.

1st Hag. O ho, ho, ho !

Lady Magog. Ha, here's an unexpected counter movement, or rebuff.

Gen. Power. Ladies, may it please you, the millennium's
about arrived, and something inspires me to attempt the rapturous inauguration.

Ladies. Ha, ha, ha, ha, ha !

Lady Magog. Hang thy inspiration, going to confound
Europe, all the powers together.

Gen. Power. Donald, ho ! If you know any likely young
men for Hymen's capital knot, bring them hither right away,
Donald.

Re-enter Donald.

Donald. Ay, ay ! I've got the likely young men, General,
but they are bashful and shy to appear before so many ladies.
Come in, I say, come in.

Gen. Power. O, beautiful millennium, great time for
marriages !

[Waves them, and then exits to bring them in.

1st Hag. Millennium, General, O, that were triumph complete as sunshine over inveterate bigot and despot night of
earth.

2d Hag. Millennium ! O, the charm that's in some names !
The lovely thought like sunshine in the sky,
Plants heavenly beauty on the haggard cheek.
Millennium !

3d Hag. Ay, neither miserable bachelors nor old maids in
the millennium.

Lady Magog. Furies, why don't you tear him in pieces
before his staff ?

[Re-enter Donald with likely young men, who stagger,
frightened at the furies, and run out again, and
Donald after them.

Gen. Power. Ho, Donald ! Couldn't you find husbands respectively for the ladies here ?

Lady Magog. Why don't you plant your nails in his face, termagants ?

>   [Lady Magog edges on the hags with her elbows and with furious phrases.

Lady Gog. As you have been paid to do, hussies !

Gen. Power. Ho, Donald ! Couldn't you find husbands respectively for the ladies here ?

>   [Re-enter Donald with likely young men.

Donald. Ay, could I, if you'd do the right thing, and lend them the helping hand.

Gen. Power. I shall dower them and rapture them toward marriage, if they're ready for so enlightened revolution of their fortune.

1st Hag. Ay, are we ?

>   [Lady Gog and Magog shriek and tear their hair.

2d Hag. Though doubtful of ever seeing it.

Donald. You rabid creatures, I have looked you up husbands. Wed, and beget buds of humanity, future citizens of enlightened Republic, in lieu of devouring unfortunate world, laid out on universal cross, for the especial——

Gen. Power. Stop, Donald !

Donald. Praise and exaltation of holy bigots or Pharisees and despots in legislature——

Gen. Power. Donald, you've said enough !

Donald. And executive halls.

Gen. Power. Well, ladies, there's a lot for you severally.

1st Hag. O, where, General Power ?

Gen. Power. Why, in the neighborhood, in near proximity.

>   [Hags approach and ogle the young men. Young men run back affrighted.

Gen. Power. I am about to divide the world in lots, to suit the Sovereign People, according to God, of Nature's highest type of law, the Enlightened Law.

Lady Magog. Europe's lost to the Powers !

Lady Gog. Lost to us ! Lost to us, is Europe !

> [They shriek, tear their hair, and show disordered mind and action.

Gen. Power. Your ages ?

1st Hag. A woman never tells her real age ! Heaven bless you, never !

Gen. Power. I'm going to donate a lot, to severally complete ye withal.

Donald. A select lot, and a choice husband to the boot !

2d Hag. O, that's rapture upon rapture ! Rapture too exceeding !

Gen. Power. So shall I dower and marry you.

Hags. What ?

1st Hag. O rapturous General Power !

2d Hag. How will he do it ?

Gen. Power. Your dower shall be that.

> [Gives them title deeds to free homes.

> [Exeunt ladies of the Embassies in wild dismay. Exeunt on the opposite side, Hercules Power and his friends, followed by Donald and Hags arm in arm with young men, making demonstrations of extreme joy.

CHAPTER III.

SCENE.—The Porch of the Capitol, the heathen, Pharisaic counterfeit of God's Heaven, universal by Enlightened Law. Enter Hercules Power, and Congressmen.

[Cry of murder heard inside of the Capitol. Senators and Representatives rush in and leave General Power standing alone. Presently a bleeding man is brought out, supported in the arms of the excited Senators and Representatives, and borne off to a carriage.

1st Senator. What's the remedy for these things?

2d Senator. Will your Enlightenment reach so almighty deep as to heal the distraction of fanatic disunionists, threatening to rend the country, or rather the citizens, apart?

Hercules Power. Enlightenment is everybody let alone everybody else. This wouldn't have happened under universal Enlightened Law, perfectly identifying and rapturing all the citizens, to complete beautiful unity.

1st Senator. But the bone of contention is the niggers.

Gen. Power. Their redemption cannot come by an intestine war, only by Enlightenment, universal, profitable, and catholic, showing the true way out of all difficulties, and doing the best, possible, for every body in present and future.

[Exeunt General Hercules Power, and Honorable Senators and Representatives.

[Enter another batch of Congressmen.]

2d Congressman. Our predecessors have lobbied away the public lands.

3d Congressman. No resource but the treasury now.

1st Congressman. See how much we can put upon the fools that sent us here to legislate for them.

2d Congressman. What is conceived in folly, ends in infamy—but never mind.

3d Congressman. Ay, never mind. If the people will stand donation of public lands to lobby favorites, they'll stand anything.

4th Congressman. If you vote for the five million lobby scheme, you know, and you know.

1st Congressman. Ay, I'll vote.

2d Congressman. And so will I.

3d Congressman. And I, too.

4th Congressman. So will we all.

5th Congressman. Then into the Hall, gentlemen!

[Exeunt Congressmen.

[Enter Old Time, and young men of the army of the Sun.]

1st Young man. Old Time, elevate your capital scythe.

Old Time. Here's work enough! work enough!

2d Young man. Pyramids of obstruction to remove.

1st Young man. O, Arches, Pyramids, and Towers of
    Babel,
Built up in opposition to the People,
Soon enlightened and elevated like heaven,
In rapturous, perfect sovereign unity
By Enlightened Law.

[Old Time flourishing his scythe, presents its trenchant edge towards the stately but overshadowing pile of the capitol.

Re-enter Congressmen.

1st Congressman. We have voted it, and it is passed, the five million appropriation.

1st Lobbyman. Hurrah, the lobby forever !

3d Congressman. What's that you're doing ?

Old Time. Prefiguring the end of inhuman sham,
Copied of Rome's corrupted'st example !

1st Lobbyman. Ha, ha, ha, ha, ha !   We'll be discovered to the people.

Old Time. I announce the end ! I announce the future end
Of capitols and of shops that do pretend
To conjure laws, when laws are already made,
The laws of vital heavenly embodying type,
The Enlightened Law for the world's highest good ;
Immeasurably rapturing business and trade ;
Elevating all the world to heaven complete.

1st Congressman. But, Old Mr. Time, what shall the people do for a national capitol in the future ?

Old Time. There's an infinite better and more everlasting National Capitol, even in view of the Sovereign People.

1st Congressman. What ?

Old Time. Heaven !

1st Congressman. That's all abstraction !

Old Time. No, not only yonder amid the stars of ether, but here, by operation of Enlightened Law, upon every foot of the raptured earth, is heaven perpetually about them, as soon as the people know it, and vote it with acclamations, but vanishes the moment they regard other halls and capitols.

1st Young man. Ay, I dare say, that's all the difficulty in realizing it.

1st Congressman. But where's a constitution, the bond to maintain the Union in future ?

Old Time. The greatest constitution of all, Heaven, a vital impregnable embodied constitution, not an external incoherent rope of sand, is yours and all the earth's in the rapturous future.

1st Young man. But how is Heaven to be achieved?

Old Time. By Enlightened Law, elevating all the people to become their own landlords. By general Enlightenment of the People, too, in universal Rapturous Universities, or Church, school and college combined, of nature's ineffable Author, Omnipotent God, ocean of vital creative rays, an all pervading ethereal or spiritual Glory and Perfection.

BOOK III.

CHAPTER I.

Enter citizens, meeting citizens.

1st Citizen. What's the news?

2d Citizen. Rapturous!

3d Citizen. What?

4th Citizen. The Queen of Heaven, and more than forty other sovereign Queens, with their several trains, are arrived in Washington.

[Enter citizens meeting.]

5th Citizen. Upon the great event, Congress adjourned.

4th Citizen. General Power has announced the millennial celebration for to-morrow; and all the city's in ecstacies, not excepting the Plug-uglies and Dead-rabbits, so reprobate and unsusceptible of rapture, and the better expressions of man's nature.

[Enter more citizens.]

1st Citizen. What's the news?

2d Citizen. Most glorious I since the Queen of Heaven's arrival the Sovereign Citizens can do nothing but exchange congratulations.

3d Citizen.   All the Great Powers already do
Look rueful, like a tree shook of its leaves;
Lean like a crazy fabric toward their fall
And final irrecoverable overthrow,
Or mergence with the citizens in business.

2d Citizen.   No rotary storm nor whirl-wind
E'er wrought so immediate, almighty change
In the world as Enlightenment, magnetizing it
To unity and perfection all complete.
Offering a glorious view of liberty
Raptures the sovereign citizens away.

[Re-enter more citizens.]

1st Citizen. Hurrah, arrived is Heaven's Queen;
Justitia, top of admiration!

2d Citizen. We acknowledge no Queen but Heaven; no King but Enlightenment that raptures all the people, as mutual united sovereigns and brothers in Diamond Republic!

[Enter General Hercules Power and his staff on horseback, severally clad in full uniform of officers of the Grand Army of the Sun, otherwise, the Legion of Enlightenment. Enter in a carriage drawn by milk-white horses, Justitia, representing the Queen of Heaven, attended in other carriages by a train of over forty queens, deputies from as many States and Territories.

1st Citizen. Behold, glory of all, the Queen of Heaven
And diamond pattern of the hitherto mean
Haggard, poor-hearted earth.

2d Citizen.   Hail, Heaven's effulgent Queen
World's perfect, glorious regulator at the start,
Rapturing it all by enlightenment
To immediate sovereign unity and content.

3d Citizen. Is that Justitia, Heaven's perfect Queen, O,
General Power ?

Hercules Power. Her munificent representative, citizens,
who will reconcile America entirely to herself, and rapture
all the haggard world together, at the same time; a queen
to join rich and poor in a perpetual enlightened league of
unity.

> [Exeunt General Hercules Power and his Staff, and
> Queen Justitia and her train of more than forty
> queens.

> [Enter Mr. Magnus Sham and Company; the chief of
> the firm considerably curtailed of his former glori-
> ous proportions; his head tied up in a handker-
> chief, having the pallid and stricken aspect of a
> very sick man indeed; followed by a drooping
> string of friends and dependents like the melan-
> choly tail of an ailing mastiff.

Sham No. 1. O, Mr. Magnus Sham,
A most untoward arrival is Queen Justitia.

Sham No. 2. Never was so fatal message to political
drovers and butchers, as that raptured one Queen Justitia is
now delivering from the capitol steps.

Magnus Sham.   Courage !
Where was a body like me hitherto ?
Seek the stage most suited to a rostrum.
I'll thunder opposition, and distract
The Sovereigns, and so destroy Justitia,
Puppet of that contriver, Hercules Power.

[Exeunt Mr. Magnus Sham and Company and their numerous friends, retainers, fuglemen and office-seekers.

[Re-enter Mr. Magnus Sham, supported between two friends, and followed by his numerous retainers and office-seekers.

Sham No. 1. Justitia, Heaven's capital Queen, has just now published her capitol message from the capitol steps.

Magnus Sham. Now behooves I address the masses of the people, and with overpowering verbiage neutralize the rapturous effect of her message.

Re-enter Hercules Power.

Magnus Sham. O thou bold villain Power!

Hercules Power. Enlightenment will be bold, sir, Enlightenment, whose mission is to renew the old haggard world like the diamond.

Magnus Sham. Fy, thou knave!
To seize so naughtily on the capitol,
And all the avenues for your celebration.

Hercules Power. Good sir, why not? Enlightenment and Enlightened Law and Government merit the greatest eclat of all the world.

Magnus Sham. I'm sick! I'm took with cholera, help me home!

Sham No. 1. O Mr. Magnus! O dear, Mr. Sham!

[Exit Magnus, borne away by his friends.

CHAPTER II.

Scene.—A Street. A rough board affair, known as the Polls. Enter citizen voters, about to deposit their votes. Fuglemen of the big Beggars of offices get hold of them and ply them with their usual crafty arts. Enter General Power and young men of the Army of the Sun.

First Politician. Vote for Stuffem, he'll give you this, that and t'other, and share the last penny with you like a brother. Hurrah for Stuffem!

Gen. Power. O Sovereign Citizens! what is't you're doing?

Raptured Voters. Voting!

Gen. Power. Ignorantly, and so shipwrecking your own, and your country's rapturous fortune; and indeed giving all mankind up for a prey for want of an Enlightened Diamond Republic.

Politicians. Voting they are; exercising their glorious privilege of the ballot, sir.

Gen. Power. Voting for the cajoling beggars of office you are.

Politicians. Exercising their glorious privilege of the ballot, they are.

Gen. Power. Ballot! great privilege to ballot beggars into place, to sponge upon their industry.

Raptured Voters. How now, General Power?

Gen. Power. O, sovereign citizens, listen no more to cajoling beggars for office. No more uphold their self-interested Pharisaic version of law and government, a hash up of Rome and Britain, deadly upon trade, business and population!

Raptured Voters. Why?

Gen. Power. Vote no pettifoggers of speculative legislatures.   Vote the Enlightened Law and Government, which soon ravishes an innumerable Diamond Republic, and United Brotherhood of all Mankind, immeasurably rapturing trade, business and population.

Raptured Voters. How?

Gen. Power. Know, O sovereign citizens, that the true law and government, Enlightened Law and Government, comes by universal acclamation, the same as you'd applaud heaven, which it is, indeed, before everything.

1st Raptured Voter. Law and Government by universal acclamation? Impossible ever it could be.

Gen Power. No, quite easy!

2d Raptured Voter. How, how?

Gen. Power. Enlightenment immediately uses up all bigots, despots, and ignorant majorities!   Enlightenment now at once, in Rapturous Presses, in Rapturous Universities, or Churches, schools and colleges combined of the whole people —conducted by the Rapturous Clergy, or ministers of Enlightenment, inaugurates the Diamond Republic or United Brotherhood of all Mankind.

Raptured Voters. Diamond Republic! United Brotherhood of all Mankind !   .

1st Raptured Voter. Why, rapturous General Power, that were heaven begun on earth !

Gen. Power. Yea, gentlemen, and do you not sigh to realize so happy heaven in the present ?

Raptured Voters. Ay, we do!

Gen. Power. Well, you have the key of it bequeathed you by the enlightened, patriotic Fathers of the Republic, who originally wrested our liberties from plagued tyrant George.

Raptured Voters. We know, we have the key.

2d Raptured Voter. But, do not know how to employ the key of liberty to our enlightened profit.

1st Raptured Voter. Instruct us how, O rapturous General Power !

Politician. How dare you instigate sedition, sir ?

Gen. Power. The sedition is with you, traitors to God, traitors to mankind, traitors to nature, traitors to your own selves, your families and your children, in the end as you will know when you abjure the devil and embrace enlightenment.

Politician. You're obstructing the polls with your Enlightenment.

Gen. Power. Enlightenment raptures you home to your only legitimate sphere. No more power in the Diamond Republic, with all mankind raptured to foundations, to one man than another.

Raptured Voter. O General Power, read us a few paraphrases of Enlightened Gospel !

Gen. Power. Enlightenment teaches that but for the haggard plague of politics and party disastrous state invention, its haggard offspring, the population of the United States were now a hundred millions of Sovereign united Citizens, a glorious Happy Family of Enlightened Freemen, in lieu of only thirty millions of distracted sects and factions.

1st Raptured Voter. Hurrah, government by universal Enlightened acclamation !

2d Raptured Voter. Hurrah, rapturous Churches or Universities of the Whole People !

3d Raptured Voter. Hurrah, every man his own landlord by Enlightened Law, giving rent to buy the property.

4th Raptured Voter. Hurrah, Rapturous Presses of the Enlightened Sovereign People !

5th Raptured Voter. Hurrah, the Sovereign Citizens united in a Diamond Republic of Mankind !

[*Exeunt* General Power, Raptured Voters and young
men of the Army of the Sun.

1st Politician. What a thundering and yet enlightened
tempest of a revolution this is !

2d Politician. Nothing but to merge with the Enlightened Citizens.

3d Politician. Well, we have a homestead and lot assured
at all events.

1st Politician. A future, raptured footing in God's earth,
In lieu of a despairing grasp of precipice,
Such as society hitherto was.

1st Politician. How fearlessly did he charge upon us all
the needless disorders of our great country, now perfectly
assured of an enlightened glorious future !

3d Politician. It is perfectly true ; anthropophagous
hashes of British law ; profitable for initiated pettifoggers,
but deadly bigot and despot blight of trade, business, and
population.

SONG—DUETT.

1st Politician.   Bravo, General Power
2d Politician.   Come we away after.
3d Pol. Enlightened Apostle of the rapturous future !
All. Ravishing perfect glorious government and law !
Hurrah !
Ravishing perfect glorious government and law !
Glorious Government and Law !
Hurrah !
Inaugurating glorious, glorious Government and Law.

[Politicians take down their posters and handbills,
and walk off singing and carrying with them their
ballot-boxes and poll-booths.

CHAPTER III.

THE arrival of the Queen of Heaven's representative, who is
welcomed by an astonishing assemblage, when enter,
standing up erect in their carriages, Ladies Gog and
Magog, who, as soon as they behold Justitia in the midst
of the splendid retinue, faint backwards in the arms of
lackeys.

Madam Gog & Magog. O !

1st Lackey. Help, ho !

2d Lackey. Help the ladies of the ambassadors.

1st Diamond Cit. Lo, the Queen of Heaven's representative

Is on her way to inaugurate the diamond future.

2d Diamond Cit. See the ladies of the Ambassadors are
carried off.

1st Lackey. My lord Magog ! ho ! help for my lady.

2d Lackey. My lord Gog ! ho ! help for my lady.

[Lackeys vociferate.

1st Diamond Cit. Let us help the ladies of the Ambassadors.

2d Diamond Cit. Help them ! Let them help themselves.

1st Diamond Cit. How, sir ?

2d Diamond Cit. Marry, sir, get a better heart.

3d Diamond Cit. Ay, for their corrupt one gives them
so much pain and anguish of envy they have swooned on the
mere view of the incomparable Queen of Heaven's representative, Justitia.

[Madam Gog, and Madam Magog are borne off by
lackeys.

2d Diamond Cit. The fashionable women are killed off
    even by envy of
The ravishing sight of Heaven's perfect Queen,
The glorious out flower of the ages,
For whom the time hath languished hitherto.

1st Diamond Cit. 'Tis pity, if they cannot look on Heaven's proxy, without going off in faint.

2d Diamond Cit. Ay, something very flagrant in them,
when they faint away in view of perfection.

[Re-enter Gog and Magog.]

Gog. Where's my lady ?

Magog. Where's lady Magog ?

Director Diamond. Gentlemen, at the capital sight of the
Queen of Heaven, your ladies swooned, and are just now
borne off by lackeys !

Magog. More deadly work of democratic upstart Power,
for which, I swear, I'll have his life, or such full bloody
measure of vengeance, as will amaze you, Gog. Come !

[Exeunt Gog and Magog.

    [Enter the Emissary, otherwise the Ambassador of
      the Gamesters of the Tuileries and his lady, and
      implore Gen. Power.

1st Diamond Cit. See the Emissary of the political Game-
ster of the Tuileries !

Lady of the Amb. of the Gam. of the Tuileries. General
Power, do have mercy on your own kindred that bear your
own name, the Great Powers of Europe, and especially have
mercy on our dear aristocracies.

Gen. Power. Madam, as my duty is, I am about to pro-
mulgate Enlightened Law, which embraced by the masses
auspiciously merges the Great Powers, and ravishes Enlight-

ened Government, otherwise the kingdom of Heaven. I shall go on, to inaugurate the Millennium.

> [Hereupon ravishing murmurs ascend from the innumerable sovereign citizens, in view and out of view. Enter General Power, jubilant Young men and Veterans of the army of the Sun.

Young men and Veterans. O, citizens, arrived is the Queen of Heaven,
Arrived is Heaven's perfect, ravishing Queen.

Gen. Power. Forth, O citizens, and welcome Heaven's representative.

> [Exeunt General Power, and Citizens, Young men, and Veterans.

> [Re-enter Gog and Magog, severally hurrying his lady across the stage, supported by lackeys.

Gog. This way !

Magog. Ay, this way ! The other way, democratic upstart Power is holding forth in flattery of his proxy, of what does he call her ?

> [Re-enter General Power.]

Gen. Power. Heaven inaugurating Enlightened Law, which, once embraced by the citizens, supersedes the anthropophagous Great Powers, and institutes Heaven's own kingdom, Mankind's Diamond Union.

Magog. The carriage, ho ! the carriage !

> [Exeunt Gog and Magog, and the ladies supported by lackeys. Exeunt Hercules Power, and citizens.

CHAPTER IV.

Scene.—A room in Hercules Power's house.   Secretaries at
work.   The Captain of Enlightened Law and Diamond
Conquest is writing despatches to the several endless, tax-
grinding, and impoverishing governments.

Secretary. Commander General Power's despatch to Louis
Napoleon; demanding him why he shouldn't acknowledge
the Universal Brilliant and Opulent Republic of the Enlightened Sovereign People, inaugurated by Enlightened Law,
which exalted in America, ravishes all the world according
to the same rapturous, enduring pattern, setting all society
in order, like the everlasting brilliant harmonious stars.

Special Messenger. Commander General Power's despatch
to Louis Napoleon, sir !

Secretary. Commander General Power's despatch to the
Emperor of Austria, demanding him to acknowledge the
Universal Brilliant and Opulent Republic of the Enlightened
united Raptured Sovereigns.

Special Mess. Commander General Power's despatch to
the Emperor of Austria, sir !

Secretary. Commander General Power's despatch to the
Parliament and Ministry, demanding them in the name of
God and the Sovereign People, why they should not recog-
nize the world-wide, resplendent Opulent Diamond Union of
Enlightened, and united and Raptured Sovereign Mankind,
every one of the universal harmonious brotherhood, ravished

to be his own landlord by Enlightened Law, prerogatived like majesty in his own right to walk the world, and enjoy it like royalty with right glorious infallible addition.

Special Mess. Ay, sir, Commander General Power's dispatch to the Parliament and Ministry!

[Enter Lords Gog and Magog, and attendants.

Gog. O wo the day! What keeps the bankers, does any body know?

Hercules Power. Nothing, but they are loath to stultify themselves by sitting down between two stools.

Magog. Everything depends on the magnificent bribe
To offer Power to corrupt him, and
Destroy him as the Enlightened hope of the people.

Gog. O if the bankers don't hurry up, the props will be knocked from under our respective governments!

Magog. Go to all the handy bankers! Tell them we want twenty-five millions to offer Hercules Power.

[Exeunt Secretaries of Gog and Magog.

Hercules Power. Vain it is, Lord Magog. I have no intention to forego and abandon my contemplated rapturous expedition to liberate Europe by Enlightenment and Enlightened Law, inaugurating an irrepressible upward popular movement, toppling down great Powers, and creating by natural force of circumstance, correct, self-supporting, and identical public administration for the several nations, become a universal Brotherhood.

Gog. O wo the day! Enlightenment and Enlightened Law
Will rapidly dry up governments tax-grinding,
And turn old Europe to a giant young
Diamond Republic.
O wo the day! Ambassadors are in a sorry way.

Enter Young men of the Army of the Sun.

1st Young man. Ambassadors that pride themselves so
   highly,
Are no bodies in enlightened future.

2d Young man. What need of Ambassadors in world
magnetically amalgamated by telegraphs, I cannot understand.

   [Enter Bankers, with clerks carrying sacks of gold.

Banker. Commander Hercules Power, all this great sum
is yours; besides a liberal grant of land out west, to forego
your contemplated expedition to liberate Europe by Enlightened Law announcements.

CHAPTER V.

Scene.—A park. Preparations for the Inaugural Celebration. An amphitheatre. Enter General Hercules Power
   and his staff of officers. Enter Lords Gog and Magog and
   attendants.

1st Citizen. See, the Ambassadors.

Lord Magog. Sir, what exception do ye take to the Ambassadors.

1st Citizen. None, yet if you'd know our mind—

Lord Magog. I shall know it or belabor you into a con-
fession.

1st Citizen. Your tax-grinding masters are a kind of
fashionable highwaymen, who say to the nations, ' stand and
deliver—your money or your life !'

Lord Magog. Ha, villain, follower of upstart Power !

Gen. Power. Individual thrones operate to abase the Sovereign Citizens.

Young men. Wipe them out! Away with them out of God's rapturous ship!

Gen. Power. No! Young men of the Army of the Sun, Enlightenment is the king and general of peaceful triumphs.

Lord Magog. Ha, ha, ha! They look terrible threatening.

Gen. Power. Yet, I'll show them thrones enough. My Lords, look, there are the matter of forty set around this amphitheatre.

Lord Gog. Ha, ha, ha! We see!

Gen. Power. In the centre is a crowning throne, approached by a grand flight of stairs richly carpeted.

Lord Magog. O ho!

Gen. Power. I am about to fill those forty and odd thrones with as many model queens, the representatives of a future Diamond United States.

Lord Gog. Ha, hang thine ingenuity, going to confound the particular Great Powers.

Lord Magog. A knave, a knave, a most villainous contriver!

Lord Gog. Who's she allotted to the middle throne in your amphitheatre.

Gen. Power. Justitia, proxy of Heaven who filleth all except—

Lord Gog. Ha, what?

Gen. Power. Satan's stereotyped Empire, Christendom; a Pharisaic masterpiece, unauthorized by Christ, whose prayer is God's kingdom of Heaven!

Lord Gog. Ha, indeed!

Lord Magog. O why, sir, you'll fail with your Enlightenment. Brougham, in England, tried the diffusion of useful knowledge with but little appreciable good toward elevating the masses.

Gen. Power. Gentlemen, Enlightenment is not political economy colored suitable to the views of England's governors, but an imbuing with God's ideas, according to his universal rapturous surrounding standard of heaven; accomplishing, not only its own diamond triumph, but also the inauguration of natural straightforward Law, Enlightened Law, achieving the highest good of all the world in God's immediate Kingdom of Heaven.

Gen. Eagle. Of this sort of Enlightenment we have the greatest hope, as the foundation of a vital republic of the globe, a United Brotherhood of the nations, inaugurated on the mergence of the Great Powers, by rapturous operation of Enlightened Law.

Lord Gog. Confusion!

Lord Magog. Ho, hurry up the shoulder-hitters!

Valet. Ay, sir!   [Valet goes accordingly.

Lord Gog. Ho, bring hither the pugilists!

[Still another messenger goes.

2d Valet. Ay, sir!

Lord Magog. Gog, go ourselves, and like Boreas inspire them with a reckless fury for the warlike brunt.

[Thereon exeunt, but presently re-enter the giant ambassadors Lords Gog and Magog, heading an assemblage of pugilists and rowdies.

Lord Magog. Hit in right and left!

Lord Gog. Give it him!

Lord Magog. Knock down upstart democratic Power!

Lord Gog. Pitch into the would-be Napoleon of Enlightenment!

Enter the Young men of the Army of the Sun.

1st Young man. I am one of the Army of the Sun.

> [Pulls forth an elastic gilded helmet, ornamented
> with a plume, and dons the same.

2d Young man. And I, another.

> [Also dons a gilded helmet and plume.

3d Young man. And I!

Young men. So we are all!

> [At the same moment more than a hundred stand
> forth equipped with similar helmet and plume.

Hercules Power. Hundreds of standards in the world, but
Enlightenment the only complete one. Hail, Enlighten-
ment's standard, that probably shall soon precede every other;
Enlightenment, latest, most perfect.

1st Citizen. Now, I do believe here is the final great
battle between the warring powers of darkness and light.

2d Citizen. O rapturous General Power!

3d Citizen. O enlightened perfect brotherly Power!

4th Citizen. O noble Hercules Power!

> [Magog and Gog lead on the pugilists. Young men
> of the Army of the Sun form a phalanx, and
> briefly repel the assailants.

1st Young man. It's over!

2d Young man. We've routed them!

3d Young man. Gog and Magog have taken to their heels.

1st Young man. See them flying like two windmills broke
from their fastenings.

2d Young man. Ho, Gog! ho, Magog!

Gen. Power. In vain you counsel them to stop. They're
mad with affright and ugly haggard hearted terror.

Enter a sergeant and soldiers.

Sergeant. Strange to see giants have so little self-reliance

All. Ha, ha, ha, laughable to see such big animals in full flight.

Gen. Power. Deplorable, but it is a fact that giants are usually a coward heap, without a nerving spark of fire or heart.

Sergeant. I reckon so, General!

Gen. Power. What is your age, sergeant?

Sergeant. Thirty, general!

Gen. Power. Have you a wife and children?

Sergeant. I cannot boast myself blessed with so refreshing additions.

Gen. Power. What's the reason? Because you cannot afford it, you'll say.   Perhaps, you do not know that every tax-grinding government is a furnace over and around the Sovereign Citizens, disfranchising them of individual sovereign rights, and concentrating them like arid particles of fire to prey upon one another.

Sergeant. Ay, I doubt not, General Power!

Gen. Power. Yet, good sergeant, and all you privates, patriotically support our government as you have sworn, until I have liberated Europe by my expedition of Enlightenment and Enlightened Law, that I have undertook thither, when all tax-grinding governments will drop away to a public administration self-supporting, with a moderate beneficial power to hinder accidents, and otherwise minister to the Sovereign Citizens.

Soldiers. Hurrah, Enlightenment's apostle! Hurrah, Power!

[Thereupon separate with acclamations.

CHAPTER VI.

Promulgation of Enlightened Law. The Key of the Kingdom of Heaven. Queen Justitia's Message and Proclama-
tion. Inauguration of the Universal Enlightened Diamond
Republic of Mankind.

Scene.—A park in the vicinity of Washington, formed into
an amphitheatre, in the centre whereof is a grand throne
for the Queen of Heaven's proxy, and surrounding it more
than forty other thrones for as many queenly ladies, deputies from the same number of states and territories.

Her ineffable Majesty, Justitia, representing the Queen of
Heaven, presently arrives, transported in a coach, drawn
by milk-white steeds, followed by Honora, and forty other
Sovereign Women.

1st Citizen. Lo, their Majesties the Queens and their respective trains ascend the thrones allotted them in the grand
theatre.

2d Citizen. Bravo !   The raptured Sovereign Citizens
hang like clustering bees upon the ripe lips of the Queen of
Heaven's proxy, Justitia.

  [Thereupon enter Young men of the Army of the
   Sun and raptured Mechanics, followed by young
   ladies with robes and crowns.

1st Citizen. Who are they ?

2d Citizen. Ladies in the train of admired Justitia.

Hercules Power. Hail, Sovereign brothers in United
Diamond Republic of the Globe.

Justitia. Array the Sovereigns in their robes of state !

[The Ladies apparel the glorified Laborers and raptured Mechanics, and at the same time cover their
heads with crowns.

Hercules Power. Behold what mighty consequence awaits
the Sovereign Citizens by unity, the fruit of Enlightenment.
A lot in God's raptured ship, perfection, happiness, liberty,
plenty of children; plenty of everything assured under Enlightened Law, the key of the Kingdom of Heaven.

1st Citizen. The citizens by Enlightenment are become
wholly and entirely sovereign.

2d Citizen. Where was ever a pageant in ancient or modern Europe to equal it?

3d Citizen. Cæsars may well despair!
Napoleon have doubts for his dynasty.

The citizens then sing the following

SONG.

1.

Bravo!
Heavenly liberty!
Gracious fruit of Enlightened unity.

2.

Bravo!
The United Brotherhood,
Rapturing ahead
Population, business, trade.

3.

Bravo!
Man a unit,
Finished like the diamond,
By Enlightenment.
Bravo! Bravo!

1st Citizen. Thanks, General Power!

Justitia demonstrates her celestial race,
Capitally representing heaven's rapturous face.
   Hercules Power. The innumerable Sovereign Citizens,
Enlightened and united by Enlightenment,
Now form harmonious unit like the planet.
                    I have
All powerful revelation of Enlightenment
Will strike tax-grinding Powers with dismay,
And scatter them like darkness by invasion
Of omnipotent Phœbus' darts.   Speak, O Justitia!
   Justitia. To all the People, I, Justitia, beg to say, you
can only accomplish individual Sovereignty through unity
attained by Enlightenment and Enlightened Law; the
thing alone endowed with almighty magnetic power, to rap-
ture and maintain mankind in harmony, like everlasting
heavenly spheres.   The enlightened unity of all the people
begets Enlightened Law and Government, otherwise God's
Kingdom of Heaven by universal popular acclamations, and
briefly brings all mankind into a universal Diamond Republic of trade and population.
   1st Citizen.   Welcome, Justitia!
Harbinger of Enlightenment and Enlightened Law!
Herald of millennium, and world complete!
   Justitia. Hitherto hindered by the wiles of Satan,
By Pharisaic creed and superstition,
Perverting pure and sovereign truth of God;
Heaven's genuine and saving love and light.
         [Young men and Veterans of the Army of the Sun,
            Raptured Mechanics, and Glorified Laborers, then
            sing the following
                    S O N G.   ʼ
                 Hurrah!   Hurrah!
              The Enlightened Law!

Ravishing heavenly unity and content !
Rapturing population ; with it, trade !
   Forming grand harmonious diamond
World, grand omnipotent unit !
Rapt, enlightened, onward planet !

    Hurrah ! Hurrah !
The Enlightened Law !
Rapturing ahead
Population, business, trade !
Hurrah ! Hurrah !

Gen. Power. I, Hercules Power, demand in the name of
God and the sovereign People, united by true enlightenment, why Heaven and everlasting constitution of God's
universal Empire should not be voted as the permanent form
of administration for mundane affairs, with Honorary Presidents in the rational, enlightened future ; in lieu of the now
exorbitant tax-grinding and rent-grinding political powers,
devouring trade, business, and population ; operating like
endless inhuman mountains in the way of a Diamond Union
of all mankind, immediately accomplished as soon as the citizens embrace Enlightened Law.

1st Citizen. Bravo ! In all the grand enlightened theatre
Not one discordant murmur heard.

2d Citizen.   Nothing
But boundless plaudits to the Queen of Heaven,
And the infinite other sovereign queens.

3d Citizen.   O rapturous General Power, proceed
To enter up the enlightened judgment.

Gen. Power. Know all anthropophagous Powers, unnatural arrogators of exorbitant usurped rights, of endless tax-
grinding and rent-grinding inventions, no one appearing to
answer my summons and complaint, in the cause of God and

the Enlightened People, why a universal Diamond Republic
and United Brotherhood should not be proclaimed, I am
about to enter up enlightened judgment against you every
and all, for all the raptured future.

[Enter Magog and his men.]

Magog. I've heard their summons, blow a counter challenge !   [Magog's men blow trumpets.

Magog's Men. There, sir !

1st Mechanic. Stop, here, I think, is a champion of the
Powers come forth, to encounter General Power, and question
the Queen of Heaven's right in the world, whether by herself or her representative.

2d Mechanic. Well, truly, fit champion of exorbitant tax-
grinders. A flagrant mountain of flesh, fool-hardy as Goliath of the Philistines.

1st Mechanic. Who's the blustering giant ?

2d Mechanic. Magog, Ambassador of Magogland.

Magog. I've heard their summons, blow a counter challenge !   .

[Magog's men sound their trumpets once more.

Gen. Power. Well, Magog, what have you to urge against
Heaven, celestial majesty, everlasting Sovereign of Nature's
Rapturous Empire, queen of humanity in the enlightened
future, of whom I am devoted champion ?

1st Mechanic. And I !

2d Mechanic. And all the enlightened, raptured world,
too, General Power. Throw down the gauntlet; I defy you,
Power !

[Gauntlet thrown down at General Power's feet.

3d Mechanic. Magog's a giant engrossed with himself,
heedless of heaven and everybody, capital creature of the
Powers, a fit ambassador of exorbitant masters.

Gen. Power. You have entirely misapprehended the summons and complaint, Mr. Magog.

Magog. I dare you, Power, to the mortal, terrible encounter !

> [Magog looks awful fierce and iron cruel and severe at Power.

Gen. Power. I dare say you would, Mr. Magog ! but I have no reckless, inebriate desire to gratify your brutal and bloody appetite.

Magog. Come·on, ye villain, Power,
And fight me, if ye dare !

> [Magog squares his fists and strikes out at Power.

Gen. Power. Mr. Magog, that's not answering the summons and complaint.   This isn't a sparring exhibition only in the sense of enlightened argument, addressed to the reason of the sovereign citizens.

Magog. Come on, ye villain, Power,
And fight me if you durst !

> [Magog again squares his fists and strikes out at Power.

Gen. Power. Director Diamond, read aloud the summons and complaint to Mr. Magog, yet ignorant of its intention.

Magog. Lord Ambassador of his Imperial Majesty the Emperor of Austria, sirrah.

Director Diamond. Ay, read aloud the summons, so Mr. Magog will have no opportunity to pretend ignorance hereafter.

Clerk. (Reads) Know all you anthropophagous Powers, monstrous usurpers of mankind's natural rights, preposterous arrogators of inherited property in earth, disfranchising great masses of the people by grasping up God's free soil, and refusing Enlightened Law, that would plant all mankind auspiciously to become their own landlords by instalments of rent; thereupon drafting numbers of the unfortunate disfranchised into armies, to be used as an arm to oppress and reduce their own countrymen, and doing many other exorbitant things to at length move indignant Heaven to put an end to you in the world, know; that I, Hercules Power, on the 4th of July, in the city of Washington, will present to the Enlightened Citizens, Queen Justitia, Heaven's admirable proxy, who will proclaim the Universal Diamond Republic, or United Brotherhood of Mankind; also, the rapturous Enlightened Law and Government suited to the Diamond Republic; and, if you fail to answer, I shall take enlightened judgment against you in the cause of God and the enlightened sovereign People, for all the raptured future.

HERCULES POWER,

Soldier of the People;

Serving in the innumerable Grand Army of the Sun, or the universal, enlightened, Diamond Union of the nations, soon accomplished by Enlightened Law.

Gen. Eagle. This is the enlightened court of Heaven, Mr. Magog; this is not a prize ring, nor yet a bloody arena, as you'd like to see glorious free America converted into, like miserable disfranchised Europe.

Gen. Trump. Respectable Mr. Magog, though no bloody battle is anticipated upon to-day, yet the most glorious decisive one that ever the world has known, now awaits its achievement.

Lord Magog. Ha, come on, Power! I dare ye to the mortal encounter!

Gen. Eagle. Fy, Lord Magog! Have more respect to the glorious occasion, the millennial inauguration.

Gen. Diamond. This is the Enlightened hallowed Court
  of heaven,
To establish justice at the rapturous start;
And open up to Enlightened mankind,
Prospect like heaven of unending glory,
And immeasurable opulence and content.

Clerk. General Power, look out, Magog's coming on.
     [Lord Magog squares at General Power.

Hercules Power. In vain, Mr. Magog,
You rage like tiger. The world's raptured away
To Enlightened heaven and glorious unity.
Hark !

  [Enter Raptured Mechanics and young men of the
   Army of the Sun singing the following

      SONG.

    Bravo, celestial
     Justice, Queen of Heaven,
    Dealing so equitable
     'Tween man and man.

  Bravo, Heaven's Queen so perfect brilliant,
  Rapturing the earth like the diamond,
  An unconquerable fraternal unit.

  [Exeunt Raptured Mechanics and young men of the
   Army of the Sun, singing still. Magog continues
   squaring at Gen Power.

1st Mechanic. Lord Magog, Titans have the poorest chance in the enlightened future. Tax-grinding Cæsars have hardly any prospect but to go into ordinary business.

2d Mechanic. Paupers have more prospect than Cæsars in

the future ; the latter to be raptured or created by Enlightened Law, the former to be equitably curtailed or auspiciously merged with the citizens.

[Lord Magog squares his fists again at Gen. Power.

Lord Magog. Come on, ye villain, Power !
And fight me if you durst.

[During all the time of Magog's pugilistic demonstra-
tions, Hercules Power is inditing despatches to his
Secretary.

Clerk. General Power, look out, Magog's coming on like
an exploding bomb.

[The General looks up a moment from the manuscript.

Hercules Power. Mr. Magog, like an aggrandizing giant, is
largely engrossed with the care of his own interests, I dare
say.

Clerk. Like our politicians and lobby villains in that.

1st Mechanic. And now exceeding desperate is Magog
with so much at stake.

[Magog continues squaring and threatening General
Power.

Lord Magog. Where's Gog, does anybody know ?

[Enter Gog, doubtful and hesitating, who finally
takes counsel of prudence, and conceals himself out
of sight of warlike Magog.

Lord Magog. Where's Gog ?   He did promise to be at
my elbow in the affray.   Call him, Herald !

Herald. Ho, my Lord Gog !   It is the eve of battle,
Pregnant with dangers like a gulf of water,
When you need courage, like a glowing fire,
To speedily and illustriously decide it.

Lord Magog. Where's Gog, does anybody know ?

Herald.   Lo, yonder, in a brown and anxious study
That augureth ill for his courage.

Lord Magog. Ho, Gog!

> [Upon the peremptory call to the combat, Gog wildly
> startles and dashes across the stage in headlong,
> precipitate flight.   Stopped by the people, he des-
> perately retraces his steps for an opening on the
> other side.

Lord Magog. What, who's the distracted thing?   Some
of Power's army?

Herald. No, sir, Gog, faithful gentleman, whom you've
started away by your exciting summons to the critical encounter.

Lord Magog. Gog! Gog! stop him, ho! stop him!

> [The people attempt, but in vain, to intercept fugi-
> tive Gog.

1st Gent. My lord Gog dodges pursuit in zig-zag fashion
of a hare, or the most cowardly creature, pursued within an
ace of its life.

Lord Magog. Gog, I no more know you among my
friends.

Herald. Truly, an affrighted turkey-hen never made
more desperate strides for a cover.

Lord Magog. Hang Gog! I'm demigod and sufficient
myself for democratic, upstart Power.

1st Gent. Truly, coward Gog would only clog you in the
heroic struggle, my Lord Magog.

Lord Magog.   O war!
Thou art the nurse and foster of true glory.
O war, war, war!

> [Magog swaggers like a giant back and forth; then
> pauses, and hugs his sword, anon swaggers again.

1st Mechanic.   Bravo, Lord Magog !
Your step is perfect warlike as ever Hector.

2d Mechanic.   Amusing to behold the ungainly giant
Pacing in vain and desperate mimickry of
The rapt enlightened phrenzy of true genius.

Lord Magog. It is sought to wither the Great Powers,
and slaughter them in public opinion.

Clerk. Ay, I have served summons and complaint upon
the several anthropophagous and endless tax-grinding de-
fendants.

Lord Magog. I, their champion, Lord Magog, do here
challenge any man in America, not excepting upstart democratic Power, glorious fool of the people, and no enlightened
soldier, as he pretends.

> [Hereupon enter Tom Glory, the Champion of Amer-
> ica, and his seconds. Jumping on the stage, Tom
> strips stark, and throws down the gage to martial
> Magog.

Who are ye ?

Tom Glory.   Tom Glory, Champion of America !
Right glad, my Lord Magog, of the opportunity
To answer you.

Prize Fighter. Lord Magog, you're a gentleman, and as
perhaps you need a bottleholder, skilled in the manly art of
self-defence, I tender myself your second for the nonce.

Lord Magog. Hang me, but the devil of fight being in
        me——
I'm bound to slaughter somebody. Here's at thee, Tom
        Glory.
Glory, look out for thy laurels.

> [Magog strikes out at Tom Glory

Prize Fighter. Magog, give up you your pistols and bowie knife. No glory to fight with such.

> [Magog surrenders his weapons. Tom Glory trips up Magog. Magog rises in terrific rage and again strikes out wildly at the champion, who trips him a second time. The giant is picked up by valets, and his bleeding carcass borne off upon their shoulders.

> [Enter General Trump, General Eagleson, and other chief officers of General Power's Staff.

Gen. Eagle. General Power, we await your orders.

Hercules Power. Be prepared to resist any charge on her majesty, Queen Justitia, by the political wolves, vultures, and vampires.

CHAPTER VII.

The second day of the celebration.

Scene—the same. Amphitheatre in the park near Washington city. Continuation of the ceremonies of the previous day, interrupted by the boisterous misbehavior of ambassadors Gog and Magog.

Presently enters amid universal acclamations, Justitia, representing the Queen of Heaven, clad in a robe of white satin, her head encircled with a tiara of diamonds.

Hercules Power. Hail, Justitia, perfect
Handmaid of God!

Old Time. Behold the proxy of Celestial Justice, Queen

of Heaven, who has waited the matter of six thousand years for an audience of the unhappily beguiled world, unable to obtain it, until at last by the grace of God and the Enlightened Sovereign People, her majesty has found it, though in the midst of considerable and unnatural opposition.

Gen. Diamond. Kings have their pageants, but here is a new thing, the pageant of the united enlightened Sovereigns; the People's own pageant that beats all that Kings have ever enacted. The sovereign people cannot believe what regal splendor and opulent unity await them severally in the immediate enlightened future; in the Kingdom of Heaven accomplished by Enlightened Law, exalted by unanimous acclamations of the citizens enlightened in advance.

Hercules Power. Proclaim the universal natural law, the Enlightened Law, as God's own vital embodying type, to accomplish the magnetic diamond union of mankind in one brilliant brotherhood, raptured like the omnipotent planet in one grand unit to pursue a path forever onward in unending heaven.

> [Here ushers arrive from the capitol who announce the refusal of the special legislative bodies to entertain the Enlightened Law.

Gen. Power. Since we cannot be heard within the capitol,
Here publish forth the true Enlightened Law,
In more appropriate and happy sphere,
The open air, beneath the canopy
Of Heaven, denoting God's munificence.

Queen of Ohio. So will every stormy revolution be avoided in the enlightened future.

Queen of Pennsylvania. So will trade and business thrive immeasurably.

Queen of New Jersey. So will man's faith in man be rapturous, and Paradise be realized.

Queen of Kentucky. So will innumerable merchants and tradesmen become like princes, with revenue more than governments, now.

Queen of Louisiana. So will authors, editors, have royal incomes.

Queen of Texas. So will mechanics and laborers enjoy plenty and content.

Queen of Missouri. So will population multiply, without crowding.

Queen of Iowa. So will enlightened America become the all-powerful magnet of the sphere, redeeming it without an effort, beyond rational example and rapturous demonstration, like the ineffable, serene heaven over all.

Queen of Michigan. So will sacred liberty be assured for ever.

Queen of Wisconsin. So will rational churches, or rapturous universities for the whole people, fill our beloved country, and, through Enlightenment thence shed, every Hydra crime and misfortune dry up.

Queen of Minnesota. So will jails, prisons, and city and legislative halls become needless, in great measure, and be modelled into rapturous universities for the sovereign enlightened, united People, sons of God, and citizens of the kingdom of Heaven, or mankind's universal Diamond Union.

[Enter Senators and Representatives.]

1st Congressman. O thou bold villain, to here monopolize the federal capitol for your millennial celebration.

Hercules Power. Gentlemen, here is the diamond Queen of Heaven's proxy, the likeness of Celestial Justice and Perfection, who is doubtless to succeed you in the enlightened future of mankind.

1st Congressman. What, sir, will you dare, raven like, croak revolution at the capitol?

Hercules Power. Gentlemen, enlightenment operates not by stormy revolution, but by gradual serene advance. Enlightenment is a long and glorious summer for the world, ripening into mellowed and perfect autumn, with God's goodness realized on all sides. To save you from all violent revolution, am I come, to offer, like a new Franklin, enlightenment as the perfect safety rod, to draw off the intensified lightnings, the leaping vengeances, that, in the discontent of intestine elements in our country, ever might in the future crowd upon, overhang, and threaten America, that is now all the waiting world's hope, indeed.

The form of government, after the citizens embrace Enlightened Law, will then be by universal acclamations, creating Heaven for the constitution, with Honorary President of a public administration self-supporting.

1st Congressman. Hi, hi, a capital tinker!

Hercules Power. Enlightenment, and especially Enlightened Law, ravishing unity, delivers mankind from all exorbitant tax-grinding governments, and inaugurates the serene millennium.

[Enter Ladies Gog and Magog and other ladies of the Embassies.

Lady Magog. O ho, ho, ho, ho!

Lady Gog. Government by universal acclamation? Hi, hi, hi, ha!

Lady Magog. Ay, when will you realize it?

Hercules Power. My Lady, in the glorious millennium that's near at hand.

Lady Magog. Government by popular acclamation. It is an impossibility!

Hercules Power. No, my Lady, on the contrary let me say, that Enlightenment and Enlightened Law, ravishing unity of the sovereign masses, renders any other government than that of universal acclamation an impossibility. Such is to be Heaven's government, for the world's future; such is to be the Enlightened Sovereign People's government of the Diamond Republic. Government by heavenly acclamation and rejoicing, without one dissentient murmur.

Lady Gog. O the Powers! What is to become of the Powers ?

Hercules Power. Rapidly and happily absorbed by operation of Enlightened Law, among the universal Enlightened Sovereign Citizens.

Lady Magog. Shame ! How dare you breathe it here in the presence of the ambassadors.

Hercules Power. My lady, it is no less true, that all the Powers of Europe, all the powers indeed, are dark intervening masses of thunder clouds, that Enlightened Law embraced by the enlightened sovereign masses will rapidly and most effectually dry up, giving the hungering world its serene millennium.

Lady Gog. O dear, dear General Power, who ever would think that you could conceive such things ?

Hercules Power. My lady, the great Powers have had their day, and a terrible unfortunate one for mankind, confounded in every imaginable shape. Is it not time that humanity had its millennium ?

1st Citizen. Ay, by every rosy, blushing indication, the morning's come, the time of the resurrection of God's Paradise.

Lady Magog. O raven, to croak of disaster to the respectable Powers.

Hercules Power. Lo, we do here inaugurate the morning of the future serene, resplendent meridian of Enlightenment and of Enlightened Law and Government, otherwise God's Kingdom of Heaven.

Lady Magog. There are no queens in America, General Power, yet you have got an upstart Queen here to impose her upon the citizens. Fy!

Hercules Power. No queens in America? Your ladyship is mistaken, and after a few years of Enlightenment in rapturous Universities, I promise you as many queens in America as there are Enlightened womankind. Queen Justitia's message is of exclusive importance to the Sovereign People. If the world is far below Enlightenment's resplendent standard, the sooner it is made to look up to such raptured sphere of perfection, happiness, opulence and unity, the better for all mankind. Now you see what a government should be; and compare it with the governments that now are.

1st Citizen. Bravo, the Diamond Republic, or an impregnable Union, accomplished by Enlightenment and Enlightened Law!

2d Citizen. Bravo, churches turned into Rapturous Universities of the whole people!

3d Citizen. Bravo, every man his own landlord by operation of Enlightened Law.

1st Citizen. Down with the laws of conquerors, the endless tax-grinding and rent-grinding inventions.

2d Citizen. Down with the profitless, European, imported traditions of Cæsars and Saints.

3d Citizen. Down with superstitions, withering the sovereign people.

Citizens. Bravo, Enlightenment, and Enlightened Law and Government, otherwise, self-supporting Public Administration by universal acclamation.

[Here enter more Young men and Veterans of the Army of the Sun.

1st Citizen. Behold the resplendent standard of Enlightenment, a sun of gold wove into a cloth of silver, emblazoned
with rapturous mottoes.

2d Citizen. All duty to God! Heavenly Enlightenment,
otherwise, the Light and the Love of God, the pure gospel,
is the Messiah whom God hath sent into the world to save it.

3d Citizen. The straightforward Enlightened Law, inaugurating Heaven's kingdom, is before all state inventions
winding into political labyrinths.

1st Citizen. Enlightened Law assures universal prosperity, opulence, and happiness.

2d Citizen. God's Savings Banks are universal foundations, secured to all mankind by direct Enlightened Law, the
key to God's kingdom.

3d Citizen. Enlightened Law carried forth reconciles rich
and poor for ever, and creates a universal Aristocracy.
Mandind, thenceforth, compose one indivisible unit, raptured
together like the planet, to fulfill omnipotent path.

2d Citizen. This is the law; God's own Enlightened
Law.

3d Citizen. Heaven all surrounding is our capitol!

1st Citizen. Enlightened Law is all things that is wanted
in the future. And Enlightenment, the rational creed of the
Perfect Author of the Universe, Nature's Omnipresent embodied God, taught in rational churches or Universities, open
to the whole people.

Hercules Power.   Come away!
All the now politicians in America
And Europe both together, do not merit
The trifling notice of ephemeron minute
Of the enlightened sovereign People, rapturously
Aspiring to a vital, perfect Union,

By enlightenment, and Enlightened Law and Government.
The sovereigns of Republic, universal,
Opulent, and resplendent.

BOOK IV.

CHAPTER I.

THE Scene is a Park.

Enter Magnus Sham, wheeled in a chair. The numerous
friends of the engrossing political chessman having combined to give an airing, as is their assiduous habit, to the
unhappy magnate, now in a fast consumption.

Sham 1. Mr. Magnus, how do you feel in the air?
Magnus Sham.   O, good and careful friends,
Nothing can benefit me, while Hercules Power
Is going about at large and unrestrained,
Rapturing with so much of enlightened truth
The sovereign voters of America;
The people, or the laborers and artizans,
That hitherto we cajoled of everything,
But the hereditary right of labor,
And mutely suffer wrong like adapted brutes,
Of god-like sort.
Sham 2. Let's try a caucus, Mr. Magnus.

Magnus Sham. O, caucus is all knocked on the head by magnetic General Power !

[Magnus' face changes like milk soured by thunder.

O, I'm sick, sick ! Wheel me back to my bed.

[Exeunt Magnus Sham, and company, the political chessman wheeled out by his numerous sympathizing friends.

CHAPTER II.

Scene.—A room in Commander Power's house in the city of
Washington.   Enter Hercules Power and his staff, Gen-
erals Eagle, Trump, and Captain Diamond.

Hercules Power. Now embark and make the tour of earth
and announce at all the capitols of the world the Enlightened
Law; the enlightened clergy, or the rational ministers of the
raptured universities, or universal church of Nature's Author;
universal foundations secured to the Sovereign People in the
united brotherhood, and Diamond Republic of all mankind,
otherwise God's Kingdom of Heaven accomplished by Enlightened Law.

[Enter General Braggadocio, introducing fillibusters
with arms.

Braggadocio. Thou enlightened warrior, General Power,
Impress us; we are at your masterly service.

Hercules Power. Gentlemen, popular sovereignty can
hardly come over a train of gunpowder; I think, only by

serene Enlightened Law, when all men, even the bigots and despots, will find it most infinitely the best thing for their interests. Gentlemen, 'tis great mistake looking abroad for prosperity. Conquest enough at home. Do not you all need a wife and a home apiece and young sprigs of humanity? All these are the blessed fruits of peaceful conquests.

While you are looking to Central America, you are neglecting the real genuine conquest at your own doors, the true conquest, the conquest according to Nature, which, when you adopt her perfect creed, will complete your happiness and everybody's else. Till then you live like a toad under a harrow, subject to hags of church, law, and state, with their crucifying creeds, who distract you with questions of no importance.

Fillibuster. Yes, General, we see the one great question is Enlightened Law, inaugurating Enlightened Diamond Republic.

Hercules Power. Gentlemen, when you know more of Enlightened Law, you will soon put rent-grinding and tax grinding inventions under foot.

I have received an invitation from their majesties, King Enlightened Labor and King Raptured Luck, to visit their United Kingdoms; also an invitation from their universal Royal Highnesses, the Enlightened Sovereign Citizens; also an invitation from their Graces, some thousands of independent enlightened archbishops and bishops of the independent enlightened rational churches or universities in the anticipated Sovereign Popular Republic of Europe, with enlightened America about to put herself at the head of the capital Enlightened Sovereign Popular United States of Mankind. So, gentlemen filibusters, remain at home and help to make one of the all-powerful united Brotherhood in the forthcoming Diamond Republic of all America, with the rest of the earth appended to her magnificent skirts.

Hercules Power. No, gentlemen ! So soon as I have done here, I'm bound for London, thence to India and round the world, to elevate Enlightenment's resplendent standard in every capital, until it waves triumphant alike over the ruins of Cross and Crescent. Adieu, and, gentlemen, plant yourselves serenely down ; America is soon God's Kingdom of Heaven under Enlightened Law.

CHAPTER III.

General Hercules Power's farewell of the citizens on the eve of his departure for Europe.   Scene.—A public room, citizens are congregated about the enlightened Soldier.

Citizen. But, General, when may we look for your return ?

Hercules Power. I'm away to unfold Enlightenment's resplendent banner in Europe ; to rapture her population, and when that is done, and the united sovereign people united in a diamond republic for all the enlightened future, gentlemen, I shall return.   I need no arms to route the tyrants of Europe and deliver the oppressed people, being I am omnipotent with God Almighty's weapons, Enlightenment and consequent power and unity.

Citizen. Hurrah, Commander Power !
Thou art the hero to inspire the weak,
And shivering with a strong magnetic faith,
And rapturous supernal brotherly confidence.

Hercules Power. I have sent a messenger with dispatches to all the heads of Europe of the utmost moment, demanding them why they should not accept Enlightenment and all its glorious issues of law and government. Enlightenment and Enlightened Law, achieving the completest conquest, never leave an enemy to harrass the rear.

Gen. Eagle. Ay, General Power, you're going on a long conquest round the world; and, since you have no army to compel, you must needs do all by Enlightenment.

Hercules Power. Enlightenment will conquer the world, and all happily and rapturously as it should be; magnetically form it into one harmonious diamond unit, a feat that innumerable Alexanders, Cæsars and Napoleons have tried to do and had to give up in haggard despair. Adieu, good citizens.

Citizens. Adieu, O General!

> [Upon that Hercules Power departs for the voyage to Europe, attended by several devoted friends.

1st Citizen. Where then will be national jealousies?

2d Citizen. Where then the bloody squabbles of the Powers,
And mighty slaughter of the unhappy people?

1st Citizen. General Power being gone to liberate Europe, and merge her, with America, all the world, into one Diamond Republic, what then?

2d Citizen. No more need of Ambassadors!

3d Citizen. Hardly any need of Congress!

1st Citizen. Nor of Senate!

1st Politician. I shiver as at sudden mortal pit
Beneath me opened.

2d Politician. It gives us all the ague fit, truly.

3d Politician. We'll lose our three thousand dollars mileage.

> [Enter Citizens, meeting and congratulating.]

Gen. Eagle. Bravo, citizens, General Power's off to Europe, by Electric Rapture, to totally liquidate the frigid Powers; by talismanic Enlightenment, to break every tyrant chain, and magnetize the enlightened world into the Enlightened Diamond Republic or a Universal, United Brotherhood.

1st Citizen. Bravo, Diamond America soon to be !

2d Citizen. Bravo, anticipated Diamond Europe too !

3d Citizen.   Bravo !

Mankind a unit, all the future brilliant
And raptured perfect like the diamond !

    [Senators and Representatives gather in an anxious knot and whisper each other.

Politicians. See the people, now enlightened as to their inviolate natural rights, already drop quite away, no more entitling as Honorable Representatives.

1st Citizen. Americans are become like one all-powerful raptured Emperor, with determination united and onward like enlightened planet, through unending heaven.

2d Citizen. Bravo, Enlightenment !

3d Citizen. Bravo, fruit of enlightenment, Enlightened Law, that roots everybody, raptures everybody, prospers everybody; in brief, transmutes mankind all like the diamond complete, in a universal united brotherhood, or vital republic of the globe.

Enter Politicians.

1st Politician. What's the excitement here ?

Gen. Eagle. O you see all glorious America united by enlightenment, resuming their sovereign prerogative, the raptured citizens are about to vote God of nature's rational, straightforward, Enlightened Law, accomplishing the complete Diamond Republic, or United Brotherhood of all Mankind.

1st Politician. You're a good deal flighty I think, sir !

Gen. Eagle. Ay, gentlemen of Congress, were not that a perfect conquest of Enlightenment ?

1st Politician. What ?

Gen. Eagle. O that's the beauty of Enlightenment, that like the sun is sufficient for the whole planet, and no more need of Senate, or any other self-interested legislative body whatever in all the future, completely raptured like a star or one of God's own perfect orbs.

1st Politician. Your Enlightened Law is very beautiful, but I do not think it can supersede the capitol and the halls of legislature !

Gen. Eagle. The capitol ! it is Heaven ! The legislature ! it is Enlightened Law, and all the laws of the highest good which do not conflict with the same. And, if General Power brings over Europe to Enlightened Law, then begins the United Brotherhood and universal Diamond Republic; then is there an end to all capitols but heaven, with the light and the love of God everlastingly attracting together all the raptured earth. When you hear of General Power again, the world's raptured; all the hitherto great Powers, merged among the Enlightened Sovereign Citizens, and Enlightened Government with Honorary Presidents of public administration, self-supporting, inaugurated as a natural consequence of Enlightened Law in rapturous operation, creating every one in fortune more or less. Yet a few years, no more Pharisaic shops; no more Rome's contemptuous pomp, but the universal Diamond Republic all throughout, and the countless opulent citizens all identical through the triumph of Enlightenment and Enlightened Law, the Key of God's Kingdom of Heaven.

CHAPTER IV.

The Scene is a Wharf.

Magnus Sham is seated in a weighing machine, having himself weighed.

Magnus Sham. Weigh me again; I can't believe I've lost so much capital weight! How much do I weigh?

[Magnus anxiously interrogates the weighing-machine man.

Sham No. 1. What's Mr. Magnus' weight?

Weighing-Mach. Man. Most awful! Five hundred and fifty pounds, a quarter of a ton. Awful! Perfectly awful!

Magnus Sham. O, my friends, I'm reduced a hundred pounds.

Sham No. 1. A hundred pounds already?

Magnus Sham. Ay! O the miscreant Power, opposing me!

Sham No. 1. O the wretch, drawing off the people, and exploding us.

Magnus Sham. O, I'm in a dreadful decline!
O the inauspicious villain, Power,
Who, with exalting public sentiment,
Has whiffed away large portion of my friends;
And that is not the worst, reduced my weight
A hundred and odd pounds!

Sham No. 1. O the plagued villain, to blow so malignant towards us.

Magnus Sham. I'll soon be all over as haggard a piece as the Labrador coast.

[Here enter General Power with Queen Justitia, and attendants, Captain Diamond and seamen.

Capt. Diamond. The yacht has her steam up, and all's ready for the rapturous start on enlightened tour of earth.

Queen Justitia. Farewell, General!

[Hercules Power and Justitia shake hands.

Seamen. Ho, for Europe!

Gen. Power. With a ship load of Enlightened Law Books for the sovereign citizens. Ho, for London, thence to India, and round the world! To elevate Enlightenment's standard in every capitol, till it waves triumphant——

Queen Justitia. Stop! Who are these in America who oppose Enlightenment on the magnetic threshold?

[Magnus Sham's friends draw revolvers and bowie knives, and point them at General Power.

Sham's Friends. Die, upstart! Seditious enlightener of the people!

[The same moment Young men of the Army of the Sun start forth, and level their weapons at Magnus' friends.

Young Men. Ha, ha, ha, ha, ha!

1st Young man. So Sham and company, political chessmen, drovers, and butchers of the people, are even now touched to the quick.

Justitia. So, Mr. Magnus and Company are reduced to such desperate straits they must essay serpent arts and tiger stratagems of springing out of an ambush upon a magnanimous, unsuspecting enemy.

[Enter Old Time, leaping like a cavalier on the critical scene of action.

Old Time. But it will not do, Magnus, you shall capitulate to me yet.   Beware the dreadful edge of——

> [Magnus and friends start back aghast as several young men bear in and present.

Magnus.   O !
Old Time.   Time's scythe !

> [Magnus' friends drop their weapons in despair, and the young soldiers of the Sun gallantly lower theirs thereupon.

Gen. Power. I am away to liberate Europe by Enlightenment.   Diamond young men of America, during my absence, ply the political chessman and his numerous friends with quotations from Enlightened Law Book, rapturing you and them together.   *Adieu!*

> [Exeunt Hercules Power, Queen Justitia, and other Queens; Captain Diamond and seamen, followed by Old Time and Young men.

> [Thereupon enter a distracted man.]

Magnus. Engineer, what's the meaning of your being here, and away from your important charge !
Distracted Man. The boiler, sir !
Magnus. Well, get steam up, and go ahead, for, truly, never was occasion of more pressing emergence.
Distracted Man. O, Mr. Magnus, your capital manufacturing works, with so much steam up, threaten to be blown sky-high.
Magnus. Back, and let off the steam !
Distracted Man. I durstn't; the valve won't open, and a devil of a fire roaring beneath.
Sham No. 1. Nothing for it but collapse of the flue, or tee-total explosion.   [Tearing his hair.

Sham No. 2. O, Magnus, how calamities thicken.

                [Enter several flying people.

Magnus Sham. Alack, I'm no match for popular magnet, General Power!

              [Enter more flying people vociferating

Flying People. Run! run! run! for your lives, run!

Magnus Sham. O my works, my works! all my political material and hitherto capital stock about to be annihilated! O! O!

      [Great explosion heard. Timbers fly about in every
        direction. Magnus and Company, and their nu-
        merous friends, first prostrated by the shock, after
        a moment, gather themselves up and take to their
        heels.

CHAPTER V.

Scene.—A park.

Enter Magnus Sham and Company and their numerous friends, airing and caressing Magnus.

Magnus Sham.   O friends!
Gone are another hundred darling pounds of
My capital weight!

Sham No. 1. High time we did bethink how to stop this rapid consumption in you, our back-bone and marrow, Mr. Magnus.

Magnus Sham. Friends, save me, if it be possible, from the haggard fate that threatens.

[Elevating his person imploringly from his dying pillow, and after an anxious observation around, dropping himself once more prone in the chair.

[Enter Old Time, seeming grim enough as with portentuous hourglass he confronts the Shams of America, and representatives of the Shams of Europe.

1st Sham. Sir, who are you that wears so sharp a face ?

Old Time. Time, Time, Time, that hath patiently waited the matter of six thousand years for ye to put things right and straight.

2d Sham. Ha, ha, ha, ha, ha, ha !

Old Time. Now, lo, Enlightenment has come to ravish and unite mankind, and merge you with the Sovereign People in the Diamond Future.

1st Sham. Ha, ha, ha, ha, ha, ha !
Mr. Time, we feel pretty secure yet.

Old Time. Out of the way ! I'm Time, now bent to inaugurate the Enlightened Millennium that ends you, capital humbugs and shams.

All the Shams. Ends us !

Old Time. Ay, out of the way ! Out of the raptured way of the Lord of Enlightenment !

All the Shams. We'll not out of the way, sir !

Old Time. You'll not ? Enlightenment ravishing almighty heaven and unity, will put you though. Out of the way of genial Enlightenment, you frigid hummocks, you exorbitant shams, out of the way ! I'm Time, all-powerful herald of Enlightenment ! Out of the raptured way of enlightened future.

All the Shams. We'll not out of the way, sir !

Old Time. You'll not, eh ? My scythe, ho !

[Exeunt young men and veterans to procure Time's scythe.

[Exorbitant Shams come together in a knot and confer.

Old Time. Wind up the ages of barbarianism, whether the abhorred and mediæval, or the now modern refined, hidden under Pharisaic masks.

Citizens. Capital, Old Time !

Old Time. Peal the knell of anthropophagous tyrants, whether of Europe or America !

Citizens. O capital, Old Time !

Old Time. Inaugurate the perfect diamond millennium, enlightenment for all the raptured future of the world ! Out of the way, out of the raptured way, of the enlightened and united Sovereign People !

[Exorbitant Shams confer in a knot.

All the Shams. We'll not out of the way, sir !

[Re-enter Veterans of the Army of the Sun with Time's scythe.

Young Men & Veterans. Here's your scythe; and O God speed the cause of Enlightenment and the Sovereign People united in a Diamond Republic !

Old Time. He will speed it ! Out of the way !
Muttering Powers, out of the raptured view
Of Enlightenment, omnipotent Lord of Heaven !

[Old Time, in a most extraordinary determined phrenzy, his scythe revolving at a terrific rate, pursues the Shams.

Old Time. Despair, cutthroats of trade, business and population. Despair ! despair !

[Enter Mr. Time, and Veterans of the Army of the
Sun of the Diamond Republic.

Veterans. O, Old Mr. Time, spare yourself!

Old Time. Despair, exorbitant tax-grinding partizans!
The sovereign citizens are soon by Enlightened Law united
under honorary enlightened public administration self-supporting.

Veterans. O, dear Time, you'll kill yourself in your too
fervent zeal to slaughter all opposing Shams, and inaugurate
diamond millennium!

[Bogus Powers and Legislators fly over the stage
pursued by avenging Time, and exeunt screaming.
Presently re-enter bogus Powers and Legislators
flying across the stage. Re-enter Time hewing
them down with his scythe. Bogus Powers and
Legislators slain by Times's scythe, fall down
right and left.

All the Shams. O, Mr. Time! Mr. Time!

Old Time. Despair, George's heirs in America! Inven-
tion-mongers, grace-mongers, nation-mongers, all despair!

All the Shams. O mercy! mercy!

Old Time. Despair, every and all inhuman stranglers of
the Lord's Paradise, which comes by Enlightened Law.
Despair! despair! despair! Enlightenment, like God's
archangel, annihilates you.

[Enter old Wives of Inventions.]

Wives of Inventions. O the havoc! O the havoc!
Made of our mothers and grandmothers.

[They elevate their hands in horror, but seeing Old
Time's determined attitude, start across the stage
in distracted flight.

Wives of Inventions. O, Mr. Time, have mercy !

Old Time. Despair, judgment conjurers, creatures of haggard legislatures, Phairsaic shops, at war with Enlightened Law, inaugurating heaven and unity.

Wives of Inventions. O good Mr. Time, have mercy !

Old Time. Despair! despair ! despair!
Every unnatural creature of exorbitance
Beneath God's rapt enlightened heavens.

> [Old Time sweeps at them with his scythe. Old Wives of Inventions save themselves by immediately falling prostrate.

1st Citizen. Stop, Old Time !

2d Citizen. You'll kill yourself, my old fellow, in your too fervent zeal to serve the enlightened people, now entirely sovereign and united

3d Citizen. A diamond unit like the omnipotent planet !

Old Time. They'd slander me, and lay so much blame on me, they that made this world an entirely haggard wilderness, a notorious province of the Prince of Darkness.

1st Citizen. Good ! you'll be young Mr. Time again, though reported to be so old now.

Old Time. Old ! I'm young Time ! I have always been young Time. I tell the congregation of devils, that I, Time, more impregnable than immemorial mountains and landmarks of ages, their end is come ! Henceforth by Enlightened Law, the earth is God's raptured Kingdom of Heaven for all the Enlightened Future.

> [Old Time here spies Magnus Sham and Company, and his countenance grows exceeding trenchant, and he elevates his scythe. Magnus Sham and Company draw themselves up into the smallest possible compass.

Old Time. Judgment is gone forth !

Magnus Sham. O, Mr. Time, have mercy

Old Time. I'm not pursuing unfortunate broken men into the earth, as your tax-maintained creatures, your courts and your sheriffs.—No, no ! O no ! But judgment is gone forth against all shams in law and government.

Magnus Sham. That's us !

Old Time. Here's at you !

All the Shams. O, Mr. Time, Mr. Time !

  [Old Time pursues Magnus Sham and Company with scythe.

Old Time. Merge with the Sovereign People! Acknowledge Enlightened Law, inaugurating a Diamond Union of Mankind.

Magnus and Company. Ay ! ay ! O ay ! we shall

Citizens. See at Old Time, with rapturous revolutions of his enlightened scythe, hewing away at Magnus and every and all other exorbitant shams.

BOOK V.

CHAPTER I

THE SCENE is a sidewalk before a provision store.

Enter Gog and Magog, the latter having hold of the former, whilst vociferous huzzas are heard outside.

Lord Magog. Gog, thou art a desperate coward, a treacherous support as water to a man in emergence.

[*Vociferous huzzas continue to be heard without.*

Lord Gog. ᶜLet go, Magog ! Let go, otherwise, let us away.

Lord Magog. Wilt thou run ?

Lord Gog. O all's over with me, if I don't.

Lord Magog. Look, Gog ! if thou run'st, this rapier shall open sudden daylight into thy confounded, cowardly and shivering carcass.

[Enter Raptured Citizens.]

1st Citizen. Hurrah, the next news will be
Europe with America's raptured away
By Enlightened Law, to unity, happiness, liberty.

>   [Gog, after desperate struggles with Magog, breaks
>   away and dashes in zig-zag fashion across the stage
>   seeking a hiding-place.

[Enter more Raptured Citizens.]

2d Citizen. Hurrah ! General Power has returned from his enlightened conquering tour around the world.

3d Citizen. Hurrah ! Old Europe's raptured
By Enlightened Law into united Brotherhood
With America.

2d Citizen. Come away, gentlemen, and witness the installation of Honorary President Diamond.

[*Exeunt Raptured Citizens.*

[Enter a messenger from Europe.]

Messenger. Hail, Lord Magog !

Lord Magog. How now, what untoward spur has induced you to cross the Atlantic, hither ?

[Gog, under continued panic of cowardice, shoves his

head among sacks of flour to secure himself a suitable concealment.

Gog, thou coward !
News from Europe !   News from Europe !
Lord Gog. O that man with the terrible aspect of
Hyperborean bear !

> [Gog, disappointed of covert among the sacks of flour,
> dashes across the stage and dives into the midst of
> a bale of straw, and covers himself up.

Messenger. Europe's no more Europe, Lord Magog !
Lord Magog. Nor is anybody any more himself, I think.—
In a moment, sir.

> [Magog throws the straw off Gog, who, finding him-
> self discovered, darts off like an alligator betwixt
> Magog's legs, precipitating that cumbrous giant
> backward upon the stage.   Then, while Magog is
> sprawling, Gog dives inside an open barrel that has
> had lampblack in it.

Lord Magog. O that cursed unfortunate coward Gog !
He runs away and shakes down everybody like an earthquake.
What were you saying ?   Europe's no more ——
Messenger. Europe's no more Europe but in title page !
Lord Magog. What, revolutionized throughout ?
Messenger. Perfectly !   All raptured, as they say
Up in the heaven, and realm almighty.
Lord Magog. The Emperor, my master, what of him ?
Messenger. No more an Emperor in the diamond sphere !
Lord Magog. What ?
Messenger. Magogland's ruler that was,
Merged with the august sovereign citizens in business.
Lord Magog. What, so revolutionized ?

[Man comes out of his store; and, turning the lamp-
    black barrel upside down, dumps wriggling Gog on
    the ground.

Messenger. You would not know Europe, now all a rapt
unit like the diamond.

Lord Magog. How has it fared with the heads of Europe,
the hitherto gods?

Messenger. The gentleman prone in the dirt there is the
capital figure of our hitherto gods of Europe.

              [Magog strikes his temple and exclaims—

Lord Magog. O the Emperor, my august master!
The great Powers, overtaken with a mortal crisis, d'ye say?

Messenger. All in contortions like their hitherto subjects.

Lord Magog. Rather like that miserable fellow, Gog!

Lord Gog. Help! O the nails, the nails!
I lose noble blood, Magog! Help!
I'm impaled. O the nails! call a doctor to caulk the leaks
with lint and plaster! Call a surgeon, in heaven's name!

Lord Magog. We would, but thy rotten carcass of a hull
wouldn't repay the caulking. Call surgeon to thee? No,
rather die like a worthless, miserable coward; a burthensome
and execrably onerous paltroon.

Lord Gog. As much account is my life to me as yours to
you.

Lord Magog. Go to! No comparison between us. I'm
a hero and the world's adored. You're a snipe. I won't any
longer speak to you, coward Gog!
Go on, O messenger, though easy to prophecy
The summary remainder.

Messenger. Your estates——

Lord Magog. Parcelled forth 'mongst eager settlers?

Messenger. Ay! all rent in future to buy the property.
That's the raptured law, as they say.

Lord Magog. Robbery ! robbery ! robbery !

Messenger. For your property, though, they've charged me here with the first payment; (offers Magog a bag of money) only three more payments, and the tenants are free-holders, sovereign independent citizens of Heaven's kingdom, as they say,

Lord Magog. O, is it thus Enlightenment treats the great land-holder ?

Messenger. Ay, sir.

Lord Magog. A plague on Enlightenment. All very rapturous for the people, I dare say. But particular cholera morbus to Dukes, Lords, and Barons.

Messenger. Magogland is come over to America.

Lord Magog. What, the Emperor emigrated thither ? Come, seek him. Gog, thou opprobrious coward and das-tardly eye-sore, don't ye follow me. I'll slay ye, if ye do fol-low my noble footsteps, to commit me before our august master. If ye follow me, die ye shall, so.

> [Magog shows Gog how he will put an end to him by sticking his rapier through a fire-screen. Then exeunt Magog and Messenger.

Lord Gog. Magogland come over to America ! And shall I be forbid to see and glory in so extraordinary wonder ? No ! though I'm reputed a coward, I shall see the emigrant ex-emperor; I'll throw myself at his majesty's worshipful feet, and implore his protection against Magog, villainous bully !

> [Enter men and boys who laugh and make sport of Gog, who scrambles to his straggling feet and draws his sword, after an extraordinary effort.

Here's money ! men and boys, marshal my heroic way !

Hang me, if I don't take down the bravery of Magog. Forward ! March !

[Men and boys form in line. Exeunt Gog, preceded and followed by men and boys in martial array.

CHAPTER II.

Enter Citizens meeting citizens.

1st Citizen. Great news, hurrah ! Great news !

2d Citizen. Speak ! what are they ?

1st Citizen. Europe's raptured bodily up !

2d Citizen. Bravo !

1st Citizen. Purged complete
Of crafty Powers, her oppressors.

2d Citizen. See already the capital fruit of Enlightened Law, heavenly unity, harmnoy, happiness and liberty.

1st Citizen. What an immediate rapturous contrast from State Inventions, derived of crafty Cæsars and Saints; gotten up to divide and enslave the Peoples; split them in warring nations, at mercy of great Powers, the exorbitant confederates of Satan.

3d Citizen. America's become an all-powerful raptured magnet.

1st Citizen. Europe another !

2d Citizen. To mutually elevate and sustain each other, like eternally raptured spheres. Enlightenment and its issues of glorious perfectly Enlightened Law and Government, and the Diamond Republic! No other question was worthy of America, of Europe, and of all enlightened mankind.

1st Citizen. What fools we were hitherto to be cajoled by the beggarmen of office.

Enter Politicians.

1st Politician. What fools we were to hitherto run for offices, and there was the rapt door of the Kingdom of Heaven standing wide open for us to individually enter and be more infinitely opulent and happy than Solomon in his palace.

Enter jubilant citizens on the right.

Jubilant Citizens. The North's raptured.

[Enter on the left more jubilant citizens greeting the others.

2d Group of Jubilant Citizens. Raptured the South !

[Enter more jubilant citizens on the right.

3d Group of Jubilant Citizens. The East's raptured !

[Enter on the left more jubilant citizens greeting the others.

4th Group of Jubilant Citizens. Raptured the West !

1st Citizen. Hurrah, all raptured in one diamond unit Like omnipotent onward planet.
Hurrah ! Hurrah !

2d Citizen. Bravo ! The People enlightened and united and entirely sovereign thereupon, are finally come to the possession and capital use of their own, namely, universal opulence and glorious perfect liberty, realized by Enlightened Law, rooting all the people to become their own landlords.

3d Citizen. The hitherto haggard earth, transported to the stars, or more correctly, into the omnipotent arms of God, omnipresent perfection, shall henceforth enjoy a future unending, rapturous and ecstatic as heaven.

2d Politician. Enlightenment merges us forever with the other Sovereign Citizens. We're no where in the future, except we embrace the universal sphere of prosperous trade and commerce.

1st Citizen. All the enlightened people, all the world
Become one raptured unit like the diamond.
Exorbitant Government necessarily dried up.

1st Citizen. Wouldn't you call this Diamond America now ?

2d Citizen. See at length the capital fruit of Enlightenment, the heavenly unity of the Sovereign People.

3d Citizen. A feat that your Cæsars never could accomplish, who reared frozen thrones on the people's frantic distraction, created by their own mountainous oppression.

CHAPTER III.

THE SCENE is a Park adjoining Hercules Power's House, in the garden of which Donald and his friends are enjoying a holiday.

Donald. Dance, citizens !

1st Citizen. Ay, we will; kick up heels, join hands, citizens, all dance a jig.

    [The citizens join hands, and dance an original reel, singing the following •

SONG.

Dance ! dance ! dance !
Citizens

Dance ! dance ! dance !
Being we are e'en
Ravished unto
Divine Unity,
Ripe perfection,
By Heaven's capital Queen.

Dance ! dance ! dance !
Citizens !
Sing and dance,
Both at once !
Dance ! dance ! dance ! dance !
Both sing and dance !

[Enter Young men of the Army of the Sun.]

1st Young Man. Glorious result of the Queen of Heaven's successful message by her proxy Justitia.

1st Citizen. What, sir ?

1st Young man. All the notorious unprofitable creatures, hitherto the plague of our glorious country, despots, bigots, hypocrites, Pharisees, including the famous lobby, are either dead, or migrating, and like reptiles making desperate steps for permanent winter-quarters in rubbish holes and thicket coverts.

The raptured Citizens then sing the following

SONG.

Glory ! glory ! glory !
We are every one
Created sovereign free,
By heaven's liberal queen.
Glory ! glory ! glory !

Divine Enlightenment, ravishing diamond law,
Glory ! glory ! glory !
God-like Enlightenment consummating human liberty.

1st Citizen. Stand aside ! Lo, the moribund Lobby !

[Hereon enter at the back of the park where it adjoins the garden, the wolves, vultures, and vampires of the lobby. They look around in blank despair at the prospect of Enlightened Government, or self-supporting administration, and begin howling dismally.

1st Lobbyman. Howl ! howl ! howl ! forever
Departed is the glory of the lobby !
2d Lobbyman. O ! O ! O ! O !
3d Lobbyman. Drear, drear, drear,
Is all our future as Siberia,
Incarcerated in frigid Arctic horror.

[Lobby vultures fall down of exhaustion.

Donald. What, and have the wolves given it up ? O it is truly a glorious millennium of trade, business, population and everything else, when wolves do fail of heart and prospect. 'Tis world reconciled in enlightened policy for all the glorious future.

1st Lobbyman. Killed ! killed ! killed !

2d Lobbyman. The field we did monopolize turned into a rapturous University.

Donald. Ay, the gigantic shams, the idea whereof was borrowed of exorbitant Rome, have been sold off by General Auction and his industrious assistants.

[More lobby vultures drop down of famine.

1st Citizen. O wonderful millennium ! choice Paradise of humanity, cleared of all wolves and lacerating pursuers of

the unfortunate, the rapturous abode of humanity in all forthcoming diamond time.

2d Citizen. It was hitherto under George's heirs, persecute
every unfortunate man into the earth ; now the policy is to
rapture everybody, men and women alike, to a foundation by
the rent, buying the property under Enlightened Law.

1st Citizen. O truly, a most wonderful millennium of
omnipresent glory, Nature's own peerless empire, God's un-
equalled kingdom, the Diamond Republic of all mankind.

> [Enter Justitia, Queen of Heaven's representative,
> her train of sovereign queens, with President Dia-
> mond, Director Diamond, Minister Diamond and
> others, followed by General Hercules Power and
> his intimate friends.

Justitia. O what a lamentable heap of slain !

Pres. Diamond. Ay, madam, but in the battle of Enlightenment, however great the number of dead may be, it is always
so much the better, for none die of enlightenment but the
deadly hypocritical creatures of whom the world cannot too
soon be rid.

Justitia. But what savage wilderness has been depopulated
to bring together such a quantity of strange and forbidding
creatures ?

Pres. Diamond. Glorious madam, the forests of legislature,
having been invaded by Enlightenment, their original covert
and predatory tenants, reduced to the last necessity of hun-
ger, are here driven to devour themselves.

Hercules Power. To be plain, madam, under whose enlightened auspices the Diamond Republic has been inaugurated, the world raptured out of hereditary abyss, even up
to the perfect meridian, these prostrate carcasses are the dead
and expiring wolves, vultures and vampires of the notorious
Lobby.

Justitia. Ho, Queens of the Diamond Republic ! Ho, come hither, electrify the enemy's dead, so rapture may abound on all hands !

1st Queen. How, madam?

Justitia. Revive them, as you instinctively know how, by tender womanly ministrations.

President Diamond. Also, launch forth on the prospects of business men, of authors and inventors, and of everybody, indeed, in the meridian Diamond Republic.

1st Queen. Ho, rise up, you heart sick,
Or else be reprobated as coward !

2d Queen. Merchants, hitherto but a better sort of pirates, now are real imperial, with revenues exceeding exorbitant government, passed away.

3d Queen. Ho ! rise up ! capital need for everybody in the vital Republic of trade and population. Ho, rise up !

1st Queen. Ho, arise, you dead and despairing cowards; now is the diamond millennium, the time for complete prospects for everybody. Ho, rise up ! arise !

> [The former wolves, vultures, and vampires start in a moment to their feet. In another moment they divest themselves of their characteristic garb.

Justitia. Bring forth the crowns and the royal robes, such as are worn by the United Brotherhood, and let the Queens of the Diamond Republic attend the wounded.

> [Enter Queens with crowns and robes of state.]

1st Ex-Lobbyman. Ineffable madam, we are entirely drawn over by your gracious sovereign manner.

2d Ex-Lobbyman. O Queen of Heaven, even we, too, henceforth
Acknowledge thee the Queen of Earth !

1st Ex-Lobbyman. O madam, what a boundless, prosperous concourse in thy train !

Justitia. All progressing together by Enlightened Law inaugurating social unity.

1st Queen. What have you to say, to warrant the honor of being accepted among the Sovereign United Citizens ?

1st Ex-Lobbyman. Forgive us, and we'll live a quiet,
True, honest life ; no more intrigue and plot
Against the sovereign estate of the people.

> [Ex-Lobbymen then bow to the Queen of Heaven's proxy. Queens of the Diamond Republic forthwith invest them with royal robes and crowns of sovereignty.

We're merged forever with the raptured people.

2d Ex-Lobbyman. Now for the marriages, that, like the rapturous spring-time, bring new hope to the world.

1st Ex-Lobbyman. Ay, the marriages ! the spurs of trade, as well as the mother of population.

President Diamond. I, William Diamond, do lead Justitia to the enlightened altar.

Justitia. I entirely glory in Mr. Diamond.

> [Exeunt President William Diamond and Justitia.

CHAPTER IV.

The Scene is another part of the public park, adjoining ambassador Magog's mansion.

Enter the late emperor of Magogland, muffled up in a cloak, surrounded by a promiscuous retinue, Magog following.

Ex-emperor of Magogland. I'll see nobody until we get to Great Bear Lake. Lead on !

Attendants. Ho, for Great Bear Lake !

Lord Magog. O dear me, I'm Magog, your majesty's late ambassador at Washington.

Gentleman. Away, Magog ! Your master's not in the humor to speak.

> [Magogland throws off disguise, Magog embraces his knees.

Ex-emperor of Magogland. We had resolved not to exhi-
bit us.   [Looks round and surveys.

O what a bright blue rapturous heaven spans
America; what a nervous atmosphere
Here braces us like the infant Hercules !

> [Enter Gog followed and preceded by file of giggling asses of men and boys.

What's all this twittering procession ? Who's the giant in the inglorious midst ?

Lord Magog. Gog, the ambassador from Gogland ! Gog, thou dastard, didn't I threaten thee with death if thou cam'st after, to disgrace me in presence of his majesty.

Lord Gog. Your majesty, I entreat the august ægis of your protection against the villain Magog, a hectoring bully, for whom it is impossible to live in gentlemanly dignity.

Magog.   Dastard !
Thine own coward conscience like a heap of water conjures
     up shapes of terror.

> [Magog strikes him. Gog dashing madly off, rushes between Magog's legs and throws the latter giant down on the stage.

Ex-emperor of Magogland. Ha, ha, ha, ha, ha, ha !

Magog. Hang Gog !

                [Scrambles on his feet again.

Ex-emperor of Magogland. Ay, he has powdered you liberally with flour and lampblack.

Magog. O, pardon, your majesty ! Water, soap, and towels, ho ! In heaven's name ! call a barber, ho !

    [Lord Magog, blinded by the liberal shower of flour
      and lampblack, is led aside to perform the needed
      ablutions.

Gentlemen. Ha, ha, ha, ha, ha, ha, ha ! never mind, your majesty. If we've lost all in Europe, we shall not want for capital sport in America !

Ex-Emperor of Magogland. No, nor for Fortune either ! Here is her admirable chief disposer.

    [Thereupon enter Commander General Hercules
      Power, escorting the Queen of Heaven's represen-
      tative, Justitia, whom he introduces to the Ex-
      Emperor of Magogland.

Ex-Emperor.   Who's this more dazzling
Than any creature I did e'er see yet
In pageaut Europe ?

Hercules Power. The Queen genius of the Diamond Republic of trade, business and population.

Ex-Emperor.   Who ?

Hercules Power. The lady, one of the queens of California, upon whom fell the rapturous lot to represent the Queen of Heaven in the all-enlightened celebration of the diamond millennium, at Washington.

Ex-Emperor.   Admirable lady, miracle of glory !
Exquisite beauty, and utility !
Rapturous exemplar of the diamond time !

[Enter a vociferous Nurse with a crying baby, in her arms.

Nurse. Good news! good news! good news! O, Mr. Magog! look here, your lady has presented you with a beautiful boy, the laughing image of yourself.

[Magog takes the baby and hugs it.

Magog. A boy, at last! O, heavenly Father of all; thou alone knowest the thrilling joy of a father in first pressing his offspring to his bosom.

Ex-Emperor. How is this, barren for so many weary years, and now pregnant like heaven, all at once?

Magog. The marvellous Millennium has had something to do with it.

Nurse. Lord Magog, at least, I know your lady was cured of her sterility by a receipt she had of——

Magog. Queen Justitia!

Nurse. Ay, sir.

Magog. O thou glorious representative of a Queen of Heaven, all pregnant genius of the populous millennium, henceforth number Magog among thy adorers.

No more rent-grinding giant, but a man;
Yea, and a father led by affection,
Like patriarch in the midst of innumerable flock
Of children, grandchildren, and relations.

Justitia. Truly, Lord Magog shall have no reason to regret millennium.

Magog. O glorious millennium!

[Exit first Nurse with first baby. Enter another Nurse bearing another baby.

2d Nurse. O, Mr. Magog, Mr. Magog! another present from your lady.

Magog. What, another boy?

2d Nurse. Another miniature of yourself; see a choice picture of your august corporation, Lord Magog.

Magog. Come to my bosom, cherub, begotten of a giant !

[Hugs baby.

Justitia. Welcome, and room for endless multitude more in the promising millennium.

Magog. O madam ! glorious madam ! Count me among thy partisans as everybody of all the earth, in the enlightened raptured future.

[Exit second Nurse with second baby. Enter a third Nurse bearing a third baby

3d Nurse. Heyday ! Babies are coming up, like mushrooms, with a rush ! Here, Mr. Magog !

Magog. What, another boy ?

3d Nurse. Lord Magog, a bountiful present of another bouncing boy from your loving lady.

Magog. More glory for Magog ! Hurrah ! How is the fruitful mother ?

3d Nurse. Well, sir, well !   [Exeunt Nurse with baby.

Magog. O glorious queen of Heaven, patroness of babies !

Justitia. If any any more toward, let them come ! Infinite room in the diamond opulent millennium !

Enter Tom Glory and his friends.

Magog. How d'ye do, Tom Glory ! Lord Magog, though always a capital giant, was never so big, so tall, as you see him now ?

Tom Glory. What has so suddenly increased your already extraordinary stature, my lord ?

Magog. Three offshoots added to Magog in one day ! Isn't that a feat to brag of ?

Tom Glory. I do envy you, my lord.

Magog. Heaven might envy me the multiplication of that

which is most flattering to me, future representatives, heirs
to my substance. Champion, I forgive ye the beating you
gave me; I forgive everybody and ask everybody to forgive
me. In particular, I beg Power's pardon. His raptured
Queen, representing heaven, the blessed cause by prescrip-
tion of all the exceeding fertility on the part of my lady.

[Enter Gog and messenger bearing portraits.

Gog. Capital! capital! capital! the millennium promises
to be very populous! Capital! O capital!

Magog. How now? Gog's in great glory, at some flattering intelligence.

Gog. But is this no hoax?

Messenger. 'Tis truth, sincere as heaven's perfect face.

Gog. Glorious news! Stand aghast, Magog!

Magog. I never did, and never shall for thee.

Gog. Go to! I have beaten thee in the matter of
babies.

Magog. No, you haven't! My lady has just begotten me
triumphant triplets.

Gog. Look!

[Holds up four daguerreotypes of babies.

Magog. My God! It can't be true!

Gog.   True as the sky
That never failed yet toward the raptured earth,
Upholding it perpetually.

Justitia. Well, gentlemen, let congratulations, like soft
breezes of June, spread delight on all sides. Since you
have emigrated to America, what are your highness' future
intentions?

Ex-Emperor. At the sunshine aspect of thee, my humid
misanthropy, like a cloud, having dried completely, I'm going
to begin to be one of the imperial merchants.

Justitia. O capital resolution !

Ex-Emperor. Ay, madam, and I promise myself great revenues from commercial pursuits. I thank General Power's expedition of Enlightened Law that liberated Europe.

Justitia. France is come over to America, too, as I understand !

Ex-Emperor. Ay, but Louis, execrating the Diamond Republic, is off for Great Bear Lake.

[Enter Louis Napoleon and French emigrants.

Louis Nap. No, on second thoughts, I'll remain and merge with the Enlightened, Raptured, Sovereign People, in the future.

Citizens. Hurrah, Bonaparte !

Hercules Power. Enlightened Law swallows up individual thrones, and substitutes unity and diamond perfection of the People, both individually sovereign, and harmoniously united.

[Enter General Trump General Eagleson, and a detachment of the Army of the Sun, with Magnus Sham and Company, voluntary prisoners.

Hercules Power. How now, General Trump, General Eagleson marching at head of the invulnerable Army of the Diamond Republic.

Gen. Trump. Flying light artilleryman, Mr. Time, had prostrated all the Shams before our arrival. Truly, but for rapid revolution of Mr. Time's scythe, it had been vain pursuit of phantom, going after Magnus Sham and Company.

Justitia. Whom have you made voluntary prisoners, there ?

Gen. Trump. May it please your enlightened Majesty, Magnus Sham and all the other Shams, who, having rapturously capitulated to Mr. Time, now express themselves ready to ratify their adhesion to the Diamond Republic of all America, and all the earth at America's raptured skirts.

Justitia. Mr. Magnus Sham, their infinite gracious majesties, the Sovereign Citizens hail you among them.

Magnus Sham. Ay, madam! Thanks to Mr. Time, I'm now a convert to Enlightenment and Enlightened Law and Government, otherwise the Kingdom of Heaven.

> [Enter young men of the innumerable Army of the Diamond Republic, carrying Old Time in their arms.

1st Young man. O here's the capital old fellow!

Old Time. I'm not old, I'm young with such a mighty offspring round me. I've just begun. O so many marriages, and no end to the births, rapture Time anew. Hurrah!

2d Young man. He's done a good day's work, slaughtered all the Shams, and took Magnus prisoner.

> [Hereon enter President Diamond and other gentlemen.

Pres. Diamond. Enlightenment ravishing unity of the People, of all the world, now quietly shelves the Shams in the museums. Take away Magnus and the other Shams to the museums.

Magnus Sham. O I beg of you, no; before I'll be stared at, I'll drop Sham and join myself with the enlightened sovereigns! Gentlemen, I'm no more Magnus Sham, but Magnus Diamond! Now it is future article of my faith, as it is yours, 'Death to all tyrants! Hail all mankind as brothers! Respect for popular rights by Enlightened Law! All sovereigns alike in the Diamond Republic!' Hurrah? trade and population! Hurrah, marriages and endless rush of babies, of all bosom things, gratifying in present and future!

O yes, I too do vote down all Shams, and take up like you with diamond-like Enlightenment and Enlightened Law.

[Enter Raptured Mechanics and Glorified Laborers.

Raptured Mechanics. Hurrah, Diamond Republic of trade and population.

Glorified Laborers. Hurrah !   Marriages and endless rush of babies !

Rapt. Mechanics. Hurrah, God's free soil, rapturous open for the greatest number of sovereign settlers.

[Enter Queens of the Diamond Republic, who favor the sovereigns in audience with a dance, and subsequently with a song, as follows :

SONG.

Dance !   Dance !   Dance !
Citizens !
Changed like enlightened denizens
Of the rapturous heavens.

Changed like enlightened citizens
Of the heavens,
Heavens, heavens, heavens !

Dance !   Dance !   Dance !
Citizens !
Shining denizens
Of magnet heavens !
The consummate diamond heavens !
Dance !   Dance !   Dance !
Glorious citizens, severally sovereigns !
The illustrious habitants of august heavens !

[Re-enter Gog and Magog, and the Ex-Emperor, bearing banners respectively inscribed, Diamond

Republic of trade and population, otherwise, United
Brotherhood of all mankind. .

Gog. Hurrah, Diamond Republic of trade and population !

Magog. Hurrah, marriages and lots of ruby babies rush-
ing up like mushrooms.

Gen. Power. What, giants Gog and Magog enrolled in
the Diamond Republic !

Magog. Ay, all anthropophagous things, without exception, merged by enlightenment among the raptured united
sovereign people.

Gen. Power. Donald, ho ! What of the ladies mated to
the likely young men ?

Donald. A good account of children.

Gen. Power. A fit item for the populous millennium.
Call them, Donald !

Donald. Raptured Ladies, ho !

[Enter Scandal and troupe, severally linked to Likely Young Men, and surrounded by laughing and
rollicking children.

SONG—*Duet.*

1.

Donald.   Welcome ! Welcome !
Even ye that once made
Scandal's irreputed troupe.

2.

Scandal, &c.   Donald !
Now changed by Enlightenment
Into fortune and content,
Perfect like the diamond !
•   Donald ! Donald !

3.

Donald.   Welcome !   Welcome !
With husbands severally;
With prattling babies, too !

4.

Scandal, &c.   Donald !
With plenty sovereign,
Omnipresent love like heaven,
Rendering our path even.
Donald !   Donald !

THE END.